TORCHWOOD

THE TWILIGHT STREETS

The *Torchwood* series from BBC Books:

TORCHWOOD
THE TWILIGHT STREETS

Gary Russell

10 9 8 7 6 5

Published in 2008 by BBC Books, an imprint of Ebury Publishing
A Random House Group company

Torchwood is a BBC Wales production for BBC Two
Executive Producers: Russel T Davies and Julie Gardner
Co-producer: Chris Chibnall
Series Producer: Richard Stokes

Bilis Manger created by Catherine Tregenna and Russell T Davies
and used with gratitude

Original series created by Russell T Davies and broadcast on BBC Television
'Torchwood' and the Torchwood logo are trademarks of the
British Broadcasting Corporation and are used under licence.

The Random House Group Limited Reg. No. 954009.
Addresses for companies within the Random House Group can be found at
www.randomhouse.co.uk

A CIP catalogue record for this book is available from the British Library.

ISBN 978 1 84607 439 4

The Random House Group Limited supports The Forest Stewardship Council (FSC),
the leading international forest certification organisation. All our titles that are
printed on Greenpeace approved FSC certified paper carry the FSC logo. Our paper
procurement policy can be found at www.rbooks.co.uk/environment

Mixed Sources
Product group from well-managed
forests and other controlled sources
www.fsc.org Cert no. TT-COC-2139
© 1996 Forest Stewardship Council

Commissioning Editor: Albert DePetrillo
Series Editor: Steve Tribe
Production Controller: Phil Spencer

Cover design by Lee Binding @ Tea Lady © BBC 2008
Typeset in Albertina and Century Gothic
Printed and bound in Great Britain by Clays Ltd, St Ives plc

For Scott Handcock

ONE

He counted eighteen of them, on the platform in their neat little black or grey mackintoshes, caps on their heads, gas masks on their belts, some clutching rope-bound suitcases, some just satchels, a few others with nothing more than paper bags. All shared a big, wide-eyed expression, a mixture of trepidation, fear and bemusement. A few hours earlier, they'd been grouped at Paddington Station in London, saying bewildering goodbyes to parents and guardians, brothers and sisters, friends and strangers. Then they'd been bundled onto the steam train and delivered to Cardiff. To somewhere safer, away from the bombs.

Even Cardiff had its moments though. Just a few months back, part of Riverside – Neville Street if he remembered correctly – had gone in a German raid, so really nowhere was totally safe. Just safer than London.

At the top of the steps leading to the ticket hall below, a group of strangers moved forward as one, grabbing at the kids, pulling and pushing, checking names scrawled on manila labels. Every so often, a nametag would be recognised and the child claimed, separated from the others and bundled away. One by one the displaced evacuees were going down the stairs, to begin new lives, never knowing if they would go home again, or when the war would end.

Jack Harkness looked at his watch. 'In about three and half years,' he muttered to no one. And then he smiled. There was one kid on the platform, freckled, red-haired, gap-toothed, ears sticking out at absurd angles. A more caricatured evacuee he couldn't believe existed.

He stepped forward to the boy, holding out a hand to reach for his nametag, but the boy stepped away.

'Oo are you?' the lad said.

Jack told him his name. 'And you are?' Jack got hold of the paper tag. 'A NEIL.' Jack frowned for a second, then laughed. 'Oh, very droll. You guys.'

The boy cocked his head. 'Gor blimey guv, leave it out, apples an' pears, strewth, 'ow's yer father?'

Jack shook his head slowly. 'You don't have a clue, do you. Cool accent though, give you that. You nailed it right down. Never quite got the East London one right, myself.'

'Luvvaduck, mate, I ain't got no clue as to wot on erff your sayin', me old china.'

'Yeah, whatever, "Neil". Come on, we need to get you home.'

He took the 'boy' by the hand and led him down the steps, turning right to leave by the rear entrance.

They emerged into the August sunlight. Parked a few yards across the road was a sleek black Daimler. The driver's door opened, and a grey-suited chauffeur stepped out, offering a salute. Jack waved it away.

'None of that, Llinos,' he said.

'Ruddy Nora,' said the boy, 'you're a bit of awright an' no mistake.'

Llinos smiled and removed the chauffeur's peaked cap, letting her long red hair cascade down her back. 'Charmed,' she said and opened the rear door for the boy to clamber in. Jack went in after him.

As Llinos got back into the driver's seat and replaced her cap, Jack leaned forward and kissed the back of her neck. 'The Hub, please, and don't spare the horses.'

The Daimler eased forward, as Llinos reached down, plucked a Bakelite telephone receiver from the dashboard and passed it back to Jack.

'Harkness,' he said simply. Then, after a beat, 'I see. That's not my problem. You asked me to locate and identify him for you. Done that, delivering him to the Hub – then I'm out of here. There's a party in the Butetown docks tonight with my name on it.'

He passed the phone back.

Llinos took it and replaced it without ever taking her eyes off the road, turning right into Bute Street towards the warehouses that littered the mud chutes by the basin, across from Tiger Bay.

After a few moments, the Daimler pulled up outside a row of Victorian buildings and Llinos emerged, opened the doors again and smiled at her passengers as she let them out.

Jack hadn't let go of 'Neil' at any point, and he was virtually dragging him towards the warehouses, a determined grimace on his face.

He heard Llinos drive away to park the Daimler in the Square, round the corner. All those resources, and still no underground car park. One day, someone was going to steal that car and find it had a few little refurbishments that the average wartime Daimler didn't have, and then there'd be hell to pay.

He rapped on the wooden door of Warehouse B, waited exactly eight seconds, and then rapped again.

The door opened almost immediately, and a uniformed young man – naval today, made a change – let them in.

'Looking good, Rhydian,' Jack winked at him.

The young Welshman adjusted his glasses, but said nothing, as always. He crossed to an iron-gated lift and yanked the door back. Jack and 'Neil' entered, and Rhydian closed the door behind them, pressing a button that sent them twenty feet beneath the surface of the Oval Basin.

Jack watched as the concreted shaft slowly went by and then blinked as the harsh lighting in the Hub greeted him. Enough electricity to power most of Cardiff, and luckily hidden from the surface – no leakage to draw German bombers' attentions.

The lift door was wrenched open by one of the two personnel in the Hub, Greg Bishop. He smiled at Jack and then looked down at 'Neil'.

Jack's heart raced slightly at seeing Greg. It always did. He was dark-haired, blue-eyed (oh God, such beautiful eyes), cheekbones you could rest a coffee mug on and a toothy smile that had greeted Jack on more than one occasion as the sun rose.

Greg was the reason Jack did anything for Torchwood these days. And he was a damn good reason.

Behind Greg, a severe unsmiling woman raised her head from a big in-tray of documents. 'You're late,' she said.

'And good evening to you, Tilda,' Jack said. He pushed 'Neil' before him. 'Meet an alien. Or "A. Neil", if you prefer. Torchwood London have such a perverse sense of humour.'

Tilda Brennan shrugged. 'So? You've done your job. You can leave now, Mister Freelancer.'

Jack smiled at Greg. 'Such charm, such a way with the guys.' He gestured towards a contraption at the centre of the Hub. 'Had a visit from Turing?'

Greg smiled back. 'Called it a Bronze Goddess. Says you know what it's to say thanks for.'

Jack nodded. 'So, does it work?'

Tilda looked up at the machine. 'Supposedly it'll predict Rift occurrences. You'll have to take it for granted, Harkness, that, as it's tainted by your involvement, I neither like it nor trust its accuracy, reliability or usefulness.' She looked back at Jack. 'You still here?'

Jack ran his finger down Greg's cheek. 'What happens to Neil?'

'Llinos will put it in the Vaults until we find out why it's here and how to get it somewhere else.' Greg looked at the alien. 'Why didn't Torchwood One want it?'

'Dunno. I was just asked to get him to you guys. Job done. See you.'

And Jack turned away from the Hub, Torchwood Three and the alien. Then he turned back again.

'Oh, and Tilda?'

'Doctor Brennan to you.'

'Whatever. I don't want to find Neil over there turning up in a fisherman's net in a week's time. If I'd been willing to accept his execution, I would've left him to stay in London.'

Tilda Brennan sneered at him. 'It's alien rubbish, Harkness. Whether it lives or dies, gets dissected or just forgotten and frozen in the Morgue – all my decision, not yours. Now go.'

Just as Jack was about to leave, he heard a noise and looked at the alien.

'Fank you,' it said. 'An' I look forward to our next meeting. Innit.'

This surprised Jack. Not just the gratitude, or the suggestion they'd meet again, but the fact it had spoken such a long sentence, and one that made sense.

'Sure thing,' he said, giving a tap on the side of his head with a finger, then out, by way of a salute.

And he left Torchwood Cardiff, or Torchwood Three as it now called itself, and went back out into the cold Welsh night air.

He stood on the dockside, looking first out across the water, then back across the mudflats that formed the Oval Basin. One day, all this land would be reclaimed, redeveloped, become a thriving modern area of shops, apartments and tourism. And there, right there, by that big drain, would be a water tower, a sculpture; and a machine would be there for a short while and would create a permanent rent in the Rift that crossed Cardiff. Then, once in a blue moon, the thing Jack was waiting patiently for (well, OK, not that patiently) would materialise and he'd get away from Wales. From Earth. Back out amongst the stars, back out where he belonged…

Except, damn it, he actually felt drawn to Cardiff now. How easily he'd come to call this place home.

Pulling his long coat around him to keep out the chill, he wandered away from the water, out towards Butetown and the small area beyond known as Tretarri.

No railyard, no bus link, no shops; just a couple of dismal streets of workers' cottages built about eighty years earlier. Dark, foreboding and run down, the houses were mostly empty. Not even the tramps and bums of Cardiff lived there, and the last few times Jack had had reason to go he'd felt… weird.

And Captain Jack Harkness and 'weird' weren't great buddies – it needed further investigation. And hell, he had nothing else to do for a couple of hours.

TWO

The room was incredibly dark – not just the dark of a late night, but the dark of somewhere that light just seemed to evaporate from, as if something was actually sucking it out, like air from a leaky tyre.

It may have had something to do with the wooden box at the centre of the room, on the floor next to a table. About the size of a shoebox, but crafted elegantly from redwood, with intricate designs across the surface. Not that they could be seen right now. But they were there all the same.

If you listened closely enough, you might be forgiven for thinking the box was sighing. Or breathing deeply. Or perhaps, something inside it was.

The box wasn't alone in the room. Beside the table was a leather armchair, a Queen Anne, in tan. A bit worn, showing its age, creases and even a minute tear on one wing. On the table, a small glass of dark sherry stood on a white doily.

On the wooden floor in front of a cold fire hearth was

a tan rug, which matched the armchair. The fire looked as though it hadn't been lit in many years – spotlessly clean, the Victorian tiling painted black, the wrought-iron implements in a dark coal bucket next to a grate.

Facing all of this was the door to the room, wooden, stained dark, an iron key in the lock. To the right of the door and the chair was a window. Long, heavily covered with a dark olive velvet curtain.

That was it. Just a dark room filled with dark furnishings.

And the odd sigh from within the box. Probably.

After a couple more sighs, a tiny pinprick of light seemed to seep out from the box, not enough to illuminate the room, but enough to break the dark mood.

Seconds later, the leather chair rustled, almost as if someone was moving in it and sure enough a figure gradually materialised out of nothing. Almost as if it were crossing from one plane of reality to another, in which identical rooms existed, with identical chairs.

After a few more seconds, the figure solidified into a small, thin-featured old man, wearing an evening suit, bow-tie, cummerbund, a small red rose in his buttonhole, as if he'd been attending a night at the opera.

Ignoring the darkness, almost as though he could see as clearly as if it were broad daylight, the man reached out for the sherry glass. He flicked through the pages of a broadsheet newspaper which had been lying on the floor. Each page was blank, yet he seemed to be reading something on it.

He grimaced at the sherry and muttered, 'I prefer Amontillado.'

The sherry seemed to glow briefly at this. When the glow faded, the sherry was marginally paler than before.

The man glanced at the newspaper. 'Where am I?'

An empty page was suddenly illuminated. A word appeared on it, scored in a white light that then turned ink-black.

CARDIFF

'When?'

18 AUGUST 1941

'What a popular year. And where in this dreary place might one find the divine Captain Jack Harkness today?'

TRETARRI

The old man clapped his hands with a giggle. The newspaper folded itself up and came to rest on an arm of the chair. 'Delightful. Queen's Rook takes Queen's Knight, I think.' He looked about the room. 'Light.'

The transformation was instantaneous – the fire was lit, electric lights on the walls were a low-voltage, incandescent yellow, the rug and curtain become cream-coloured, and some framed pictures blurred into existence along the walls.

Photographs, mostly monochrome, showing Cardiff over the previous fifty years.

'That's better. If I'm going to be in this dimension for a while, I might as well be comfortable.' He bent over and scooped up the box – his body as supple as that of a man a third his apparent age.

He crossed to one of the photos.

'That is 1923, if I recall,' he said to the box. 'And there, in that ridiculous coat, with that smug expression – there is our target.' He patted the lid of the box. 'Jack Harkness he calls himself. Not his real name, of course, but a guise he once adopted and has continued to use. To all intents and purposes, it is whom he believes himself to be. And you and I shall have some fun with him.'

He crossed to another picture. Again Jack, this time dated 1909; he was inside a railway carriage in Pakistan, with a troop of soldiers, laughing. 'Take a good look at our enemy,' the old man purred. 'This is going to be a long game with a very unpleasant outcome.'

From within the box, a louder sigh than before emerged, and another flicker of harsh white light seeped from the crack between its lid and base.

The old man nodded slowly. 'Yes, the God-slayer. And we really don't like him much, do we?'

The box sighed again.

The man clicked his fingers, and the newspaper flipped open to a blank page.

'Send a message: My dearest Doctor Brennan. Matilda. My respects to you and Torchwood. The time has come to rid ourselves of the vermin that calls itself Harkness. File TW3/87/BM. Read it and follow the instructions. Your servant, as always, Bilis Manger, Esquire.'

The newspaper closed, and the old man smiled.

'It won't work, of course. But it will be an amusing diversion, a chance to see how alert the good Captain is.'

He sat back in the chair, sipped more sherry and suddenly yanked open the lid of the box. A massive flurry of bright, fierce halogen white light almost roared out of the box, straight up, through the ceiling and was gone.

And Bilis Manger laughed as he imagined the trauma he was about to inflict, indirectly and untraceably of course, on his… nemesis.

'Nemesis? Oh I like that,' he said to the newspaper. 'I would have settled for "enemy". "Mortal foe", even. But "nemesis" – oh, but that's delicious.'

Jack Harkness stood at the end of a long road. At the far end was a huge brick wall, creating a cul-de-sac of Wharf Street. Off Wharf Street, four other roads to the left. The right of Wharf Street was just a solid row of Victorian terraces.

The four roads were also lined with identical two-up, two-down terraces. All workers' cottages, built for the dockworkers in 1872. Back then, the land had been owned by one of the local businessmen, Gideon ap Tarri, who wanted his men well housed with their wives and kids.

At the other end of the four side roads, a street identical to Wharf Street called Bute Terrace.

Six streets of houses, creating a neat square of land.

And all the houses empty. Just as they had been in 1902 when he'd first been drawn here. And all the other times. 1922 – that'd been a good year. And in 1934, that old woman who threw things at him…

Unchanging. No sign of wear and tear. Just… there.

Jack was about to step forward when something that

hadn't happened on his previous incursions suddenly occurred.

A dog, a small brown cocker spaniel, lolloped towards Wharf Street from behind him, panting slightly. It brushed past his leg and into Wharf Street. Momentarily it stopped and cocked its head, as if listening, Jack thought. Hearing something on a frequency that dogs can but humans can't. Then it carried on moving, and then turned left into the second linking road. Jack had no idea what the street was called; if it had a sign, it was on the facia he couldn't see from where he stood.

The dog was gone, completely out of his field of vision, so he moved left to look down Bute Terrace. The dog didn't re-emerge, so he assumed it had found something to amuse itself with in the side road.

Anywhere else, of course, he might just have wandered in to see what the dog was doing.

But this tiny block of streets known as Tretarri was off-limits to Jack. It always had been. Ever since 1902, when he'd first stumbled on it, drunkenly one night. (Oh, that was a good night. That showgirl. And the sailor. Together…) He'd tried going in but had woken up flat on his back, exactly where he stood now. And, for the next two days, he'd played host to King Hangover of the Hangover People.

Same on his other visits – he physically could not get into Tretarri. If he tried, he felt sick.

He stepped forward. Nope, tonight was no different, the nausea was wrenched up from the pits of his gut in a split second – maybe a bit stronger, a bit more nauseous, but always the same sensations. He tried to ignore it, to force himself forward. If he was going to throw up, so what? He was still going to try.

He put an arm out but, just as he'd found the last time, something stopped him. Like a barrier – an invisible barrier.

He tried to fight the wave of hot and cold washing over him, tried to ignore the churning in his stomach. He was Jack Harkness, fifty-first-century Time Agent. He'd fought monsters for God's sake. How could a crappy little block of streets in one city on Earth give him this much grief?

Then he staggered back.

'I give up,' he muttered to no one in particular.

One day, he'd break through this. It was a mystery, and Jack didn't much like mysteries. Well, not insoluble ones. Not insoluble ones that made him want to bring his lunch up. And yesterday's lunch. And probably the last week's worth of lunches.

He turned away from Bute Terrace and tried to focus on that party going on down by the docks.

But no, even thinking about drinking, gambling, girls and boys couldn't convince him to head there.

He needed rest. Sleep.

And annoyingly, like last time, he knew it'd be three days before he'd be fit and ready again.

He wandered into the darkness, trying not to stagger and lean against the lamp-posts as he headed back to his den.

If he'd taken one last look back, he would have seen the spaniel standing at the edge of the street, its eyes glowing bright with an unearthly white halogen light. He might have seen what could also only be described as a smile on its face.

But normal, Earth-based dogs can't smile, so he'd have dismissed that as a by-product of his nausea.

Four days later, he was back at Torchwood Three.

His defences were up immediately. Rhydian wasn't on reception duty, but unconscious on the floor, his breathing shallow but regular. Jack sniffed his breath – Rhydian had been drugged then.

He went down into the Hub.

Turing's Rift predictor was wrecked, bits of it strewn about the floor, and a dark, charred hole at its heart.

Of Tilda Brennan, Llinos King or Greg Bishop, no sign.

Tilda's office, far side, to the right of the Torchwood train station sign, was empty. Drawing his Webley, gripping it in both hands, Jack expertly explored the Hub, checking the walkway that ringed the walls, the Committee Room at 9 o'clock to Tilda's office, on that walkway, and then looked down into the sterile Autopsy Room.

Nothing.

He crossed under the Committee Room to the steps at the back of the Hub, glancing into the Interrogation Room. Llinos was lying across the table.

He was in there in seconds, checking Llinos' neck for a pulse. Faint, but there.

Both Rhydian and Llinos, alive but unconscious. Why?

He took the steps down into the bowels of the

Torchwood base, leading to a series of interlinked tunnels and passageways. To one side, he passed the Vaults where alien prisoners were kept. Nothing.

He went further, down a few steps to the basement area, a vast room of nothing but filing cabinets – details of Torchwood incidents, staff and records going back to its inception in 1879.

Around the corner, the huge Victorian morgue, rows of wooden doors hiding... whatever. He was never comfortable down there. As a man who couldn't die, being in close proximity to those that had, made him... uncomfortable.

There was a noise, a whisper.

'Jack.'

It had come from the direction of the Vaults, and Jack eased himself along the tunnels back there.

'Greg?'

Revolver ready, he went into the Vaults, aiming rapidly into each cell. Empty until he reached the last one. The alien he'd got from the railway station, dissected, its face contorted in agony, spread-eagled on the floor, entrails everywhere.

'Jack...'

He swung around.

Greg was in the doorway, his face swollen and bloodied, his right arm (his gun arm, Jack knew) twisted at an angle, clearly broken painfully in at least two places. His beautiful blue eyes were staring at Jack in silent apology.

But the most surprising thing wasn't Greg. It was Tilda

Brennan, holding Greg in front of her as a shield, a pistol jammed against his forehead.

She was holding Greg in an arm-lock around the throat, and clutching a diary of some sort.

'You couldn't just sod off and leave us alone, could you Jack?' she spat. 'This is your fault.'

Jack shrugged and threw a look at 'Neil' the alien. 'What did you learn from that?'

Tilda snorted. 'That whatever race that piece of crap is from, they're easily stopped.'

'Is that what Torchwood One wanted?'

'I'm not working for Torchwood any more,' she said quietly.

'Kinda guessed that,' Jack replied, keeping the Webley aimed straight at her, but with an eye on her twitchy trigger finger.

He knew that, if he fired, there'd still be that split second, that moment when the noise of the Webley could startle her enough that she'd fire too, spreading Greg's brain across the room just as his bullet did the same to hers.

He wasn't going to take that risk – he didn't owe Torchwood enough for that.

But he owed Greg.

'So, who?'

By way of an answer, she gasped – and her eyes suddenly flared with a bright white light, burning harshly.

He could almost hear the roar.

Or was it a… sigh of some sort. A sigh of contentment, as if something had been released.

But her gun was still pressed into Greg's temple.

Damn.

'One day, Jack,' she said, but the voice wasn't hers, it was... distorted, hollow. 'One day, you'll understand all this. I'm the messenger, Jack. Just the messenger.'

And the lights in her eyes went as suddenly as they'd arrived – and Tilda's concentration faltered for a second.

As her arm relaxed a fraction, she clearly realised her mistake.

Her finger began to pull the trigger and Jack had no choice.

The Webley retorted, twice, and Tilda's head exploded.

Her dead finger continued on its trajectory and her pistol fired – uselessly into the wall as Greg fell backwards with Tilda's body as she dropped.

Jack was at his side in a second, and the young man wrenched himself free of the woman and fell into Jack's waiting arms, huge sobs racking his body.

Jack held him tight, rocking back and forth slightly, both of them in shock. He wasn't sure how long they stayed like that, but they only parted when the flame-haired Llinos put her head around the corner of the Vaults, pistol drawn.

She looked at Jack and Greg, and then took in Tilda Brennan's body.

'Check on Rhydian,' Jack commanded, and Llinos ran away to find her comrade.

'This,' Jack whispered quietly into Greg's ear, trying to lighten the mood, 'is why I will never work full-time for Torchwood.'

Greg just looked up into Jack's eyes and kissed him hard, their tongues finding each other's mouths in passion, relief and savage gratitude.

They parted after a few moments, and Jack checked Greg's arm.

'She tricked me,' Greg said quietly. 'I found the alien like that, objected, and she said someone must be in the Hub. As I went to get a weapon, she jumped me. I was surprised, she'd done my arm in before I could react. I'm sorry.'

Jack shook his head. 'Sorry, my ass. You've got nothing to apologise for – but you need to let Torchwood London know something took her over, possessed her.'

'From the alien?' asked Greg, pointing with his good arm at the dissected 'Neil'.

Jack considered this, but something about that explanation didn't ring true.

Greg reached out for the diary Tilda had dropped and drew it towards him, as Jack propped him up against the wall of the nearest cell door.

Llinos and Rhydian came in, both alert, ready for anything, despite their recent unconsciousness.

This was a good team, Jack thought. They deserved better than Tilda Brennan's betrayal, possessed or not.

He'd always had doubts about her.

Rhydian grabbed a blanket from one of the cells, draping it over Tilda's body as Llinos and Greg flicked through the diary.

'Rhydian, painkillers for Greg's arm, now.'

'Yes sir,' the young officer replied and headed back out.

Greg was frowning, and not with the pain or shock.

'What's up?' Jack asked.

Greg held the diary up. The double-page spread was blank.

'They're all like that,' Llinos said. 'It's an empty book.' She stood up and looked at Jack. 'What do you think?'

'Hey, don't ask me,' he said.

And they both turned as Greg swore.

A white light, roughly Greg-shaped, surrounded him.

Jack reached forward, but suddenly his guts seemed to be on fire – the same feeling he'd felt at Tretarri.

He hit the floor in a second, hearing his own voice yelling in fury, as Greg vanished with one final scream of pain, and the bright light flared and winked out.

'Greg!' Llinos shouted pointlessly.

Jack was staring, not where Greg had been, but at the diary.

In flame-orange letters, scored across the previously blank pages were words:

REVENGE, JACK. REVENGE FOR THE FUTURE.

And then the diary erupted into flame and would have been ash in seconds if Llinos hadn't stamped on it and put the fire out.

'Did… did you see that?' Llinos asked, reaching down for the charred book.

Jack nodded dumbly. Greg had been taken. In revenge. For something Jack hadn't done. Yet.

THREE

'What about this one, Susi?'

Susan Sharma took the flyer from Jan Arwyn's out-tray and glanced down at it. 'No, don't think so, that's a single clown doing kiddie parties.' She looked across at the girls in the office. It was a big open-plan office; it had originally had loads of walls, but they'd been demolished a few years back to create a 'workspace environment'. It housed about twelve of them, here at City Hall, trying to keep the Mayor and his staff happy and administered.

But not financed. Oh no, Finance were on another floor. They had carpets. And walls. And a kitchen to themselves.

They all hated Finance down here in Admin.

'We need to book a big group, right?' Susi said, remembering the task at hand. 'It's expensive if we go for lots of solos and smaller groups, and the Mayor's lot will have heart attacks if we spend too much. It's just got to be enough to fill the streets.' She smiled at Jan. 'Sorry, love, keep looking.'

Jan pointed at the memo pinned to the wall. 'We haven't got long though, have we? I mean, the Office want it sorted by tonight.'

Susi sighed. 'I know. How difficult is it to find people? I can't believe it.'

'What exactly do you need?' asked Tom, the water-cooler guy, as he wandered over with two empty containers. 'And can I just say, you lot don't half get through this stuff.'

Jan smiled at Tom – Susi thought she quite liked him. Awww.

'You ever seen that Derren Brown bloke? Or David Blaine, when he was good? All that misdirection, card-tricks, word-play? That sort of thing. But about twenty of them. And some clowns, and those awful statue people—'

'Awful what?'

'Oh you know,' Susi said. 'Those weirdoes that paint themselves silver and pretend to be angels or Charlie Chaplin. Then they move suddenly, and sixty kids wee themselves on the spot.'

'Oh,' said Tom. 'Can't help you there. But my mate's a clown – on so many levels, I say – and he'd do it. Free, I reckon, cos he's starting out.'

Jan looked up at Susi. 'Free? I like free. Free is good.'

'So if Tom can give us a clown, and there's that guy with the dancing dog…'

Even as she said it, she could picture the Mayor's face. Well, the Mayor's secretary's face actually – Susi couldn't remember the last time she'd actually spoken to the Mayor himself.

The secretary would look at her in that waspish way he always did and repeat slowly 'the dancing dog…'

And he'd be right. This was going to be a disaster.

'What we really need – no disrespect to your friend, Tom – is one company that can supply the lot,' she said. 'Street Parties R Us.'

God, Susi thought, maybe she should set that up herself. It'd get her out of this dead-end job. She'd make a fortune, all those posh families in Roath in the summer…

She was distracted suddenly when a motorcycle courier walked in, helmet on.

Before she had a chance to ask him to remove it (why hadn't reception done that? Indeed, why was the courier up here anyway?), he held out an envelope.

'Susan Sharma?' he said, muffled by the helmet.

'That's me,' Susi took the envelope and started to open it. She looked up to say thanks, but the courier was gone.

'Wonder what he looked like under that leather,' Jan giggled to one of the other girls. 'Looked good with it on! How tight were those leather trousers?'

The other girl nodded. 'You couldn't just see he was a big boy, you could guess his religion!!'

They burst into cackles of laughter.

Tom, sensing he was no longer the centre of Jan's world, coughed and wandered out, managing to crash one of the empty water containers into the door, making his exit as undignified as possible.

Susi shook her head and looked at the contents of the envelope.

STREET PARTY SOLUTIONS
Having a party, but don't know who to hire?
Come to us, the UK's leading supplier every kind of entertainer to
keep children, adults and those in-between happy for hours.

Card tricksters

Mimes

Balloon shapers

Wurlitzer and accordion players

Clowns

Illusionists

Caricaturists

Trick cyclists

Living statues

And loads more!

You tell us what you need, where and when.

One phone call, and we'll do the rest.

GREAT RATES

We are a new, young company,
so we want to impress.

SPECIAL INTRODUCTORY OFFER

Call or email and quote this ref:
08/TT/45564478/BM

There was a phone number at the bottom, a Cardiff number. Susan smiled. Her pleas had been answered. Call or email? Oh, let Jan decide.

She passed the flyer over. 'Jan, look at this. I think our Tretarri problem has just been solved! How cool is that?'

FOUR

Ianto Jones breathed hard on the glass and used a handkerchief – burgundy, same as his shirt – to clean the SUV's wing mirror.

Today, he'd chosen to park it in the space marked PRIVATE, on the lowest level of the underground car park, beneath the Wales Millennium Centre in the Bay, right next to the Hub.

Not that anyone in the WMC knew that, any more than they knew that the door marked private with absolutely no handles, locks, etc led into the winding corridors threaded through the Torchwood base.

Ianto looked up as a man in a suit walked through the car park, heading towards a nice BMW parked in Bay 18.

Colin Rees: 38; wife Joan; two children. Moved to Cardiff in June 2007 from Llanfoist, because he'd taken up a job in the new Welsh Assembly building in the Bay. He earned £59,000 plus bonuses, liked Joan Armatrading, Macy Gray and Mary J Blige, and had recently bought his youngest, a girl called Tarryn, a pony, and his son Sean an X-Box 360. They'd be enjoying birthdays in September and October respectively.

Ianto prided himself on knowing things like that. It was his job. He knew everything about everyone who regularly came into contact with the SUV in whichever of the regular parking places he used.

'Morning Mr Jones,' Rees called out. 'How're the tourists?'

Ianto was known to everyone in the Bay as the man who ran the Cardiff Bay tourist information shop in Mermaid Quay, just by the jetties.

It was a good cover story.

'Great, thank you. How's Joan?'

'Oh, so-so. Summer cold, hay fever, the works. Moaning, as always. Women, eh?'

'Oh yes, absolutely,' Ianto called back cheerfully.

Rees got into his car and seconds later was heading out to the streets above.

Ianto blew air out of his cheeks and walked over to the CCTV camera that pointed into the car park, by the handleless door.

He stared straight into it and, a second later, the optical recognition software activated the time-delay lock. With a dull click, the door opened.

Ianto had eight seconds to get in before it locked again. A deadbolt seal inside would freeze the CCTV camera systems, and it would be six hours before the door could be unfrozen.

Once past the door, he pushed it gently shut, listening to make sure it locked. He started up the short stairway into the corridors, walked down a couple until the glow of light ahead told him he was nearing the Weapons Room.

He activated another optical system, and the door slid soundlessly open, he walked past the impressive array of weapons (how many fingers did you need to operate that one?) and into the Hub.

It was empty – the rest of the team were downstairs in the Boardroom, nestled amongst the endless winding corridors that had been carved out of the rock beneath Cardiff Bay a long, long time ago.

Ianto was proud of the new Boardroom – he and Toshiko had renovated it (from a plan of Jack's, of course) when the old Boardroom in the Hub had simply got too small. And he'd been fed up with always wiping handprints off the old glass walls.

This new room was wood-lined, with steel struts to support it.

Once upon a time it had had another use, he was sure, but he had no idea what. It didn't feature on any Hub blueprints. It just… was.

Moments later, he was outside the room. He straightened his already perfectly straight tie and strode purposefully through the door.

Jack was giving a briefing. Standing there, blue shirt, braces, flannelled slacks, hair immaculate (how did he do that?). But his face – a scowl. Not a Happy Jack today then.

'And another thing,' he growled as Ianto wandered in,

'where's the coffee? Is it too much to ask for coffee at the start of a briefing?'

Ianto never even broke his stride, just turned left, pulled open a side door, revealing a small area replete with jugs, mugs and a mini coffee-maker, a sort of dwarf version of the ensemble upstairs in the Hub.

Before Jack had even got his next sentence out, a hot mug of his favourite blend (and no, Ianto was never going to tell anyone what that was) was in front of him.

Owen Harper coughed slightly, and looked meaningfully at Ianto. With a sigh, Ianto glanced across at Gwen Cooper and Toshiko Sato.

And yes, their eyes all said, they wanted refreshments too.

Moments later, everyone was drinking, and Jack's mood seemed significantly lighter.

'OK guys, Ianto's done his bit – all say thank you to Ianto.'

They did. In very dull, deadpan voices, like schoolchildren thanking a policeman who'd given them road safety tips at morning assembly.

But he nodded as if taking applause. 'I aim to serve.'

Jack waved him to a seat. 'Now then, I have to go away for a few days. And yes,' he looked at Gwen, anticipating her next question, 'I will have my mobile with me at all times. And no, I'm not disappearing to the far ends of the Earth. I just need… some leave.'

Owen shrugged. 'Cool. Take Ianto with you.'

'Why?'

'I want to take the SUV out for a spin, off-road, really ramp up the gears and speed and get it caked in mud.'

'Why,' Ianto repeated, 'would you want to do that?'

'Because,' Owen leaned in conspiratorially, 'it'd piss you off and I couldn't bear to do that if you were around. Even I'm not that cruel.'

'OK guys,' Jack said quickly. 'Overlooking Owen's testosterone-inspired madness – remember what happened last time, Owen?'

Ianto looked straight at Jack. Then Owen. 'Last time? There's been a "last time"?'

'Couple of last times,' Owen replied.

'I was glad you weren't around,' Toshiko added. 'It was very… muddy.'

'Muddy?'

Gwen touched Ianto's arm gently. 'I think they told you it was alien slime from a meteor crash. But it wasn't.'

'No,' Ianto said darkly. 'It was just mud.'

'And you scraped it off beautifully, and gave it to me to test,' Toshiko added.

'And she did all those tests, trying to find Cortellian nucleotides.' Owen grabbed Ianto's unmoving arm. 'Sorry mate, but it was dead funny at the time.'

Toshiko fiddled with her glasses, so as not to catch Ianto's eye. 'Sorry Ianto. We didn't know when to stop. But it was very… well, yes, funny.'

Ianto nodded, staring at his team. His friends. And smiled – inwardly.

Revenge would be so sweet…

Jack cleared his throat, bringing them back to the matter at hand. 'Now, I've checked my diary – well, the half-dozen scraps of paper on my desk I pretend represents a diary – and there's nothing much going on. Tosh, keep going with those upgrades to the Hub defences – we've had too many uninvited guests lately. Owen, call me if the Tammarok eggs hatch, I want to be here for that. Ianto, we need more Weevil spray. And Gwen… Gwen, say hi to Rhys and go sort out a venue for that wedding. You have four days. Cos when I'm back, no more wedding talk for, oh, at least a week.'

He grinned at her, and she smiled back, saluting him.

Jack reached behind him to grab his Air Force Blue greatcoat from the back of the chair, winked at Ianto and walked out of the boardroom.

There was a brief pause, and then Gwen broke the ice. 'Right. OK. Well. Things to do.'

'Oi.' Owen pointed at Gwen, but looked at Toshiko and Ianto. 'Who put her in charge?'

Toshiko frowned. 'Umm, when Jack's not here, Gwen always—'

'Yeah,' said Owen, 'but she's been told to go and arrange a wedding. Can't do that in the Hub.' He smiled a rare genuine Owen smile at Gwen. 'Go on, get off. The three of us will protect the world from the aliens for a few more hours.'

Gwen didn't hesitate. 'Thanks, guys. But call me if you need to. Mobile's always on.'

And she was gone.

Ianto looked at the other two. 'So. The SUV. Mud. Not Cortellian biomass?'

Toshiko pointed at Owen. 'It was his idea. All of it. His. Not mine.'

Owen gazed back at Ianto. 'Me? Come on, mate, what do I know about alien DNA… I mean, I… Nah, that's never going to work, is it?'

Ianto shook his head slowly. And then grinned. 'Never mind. Good joke.' And he got up, straightened his perfectly straight tie again and wandered out of the room, hovering outside the door just long enough to hear Toshiko ask Owen:

'What did he mean? "Never mind"? Owen?'

'Dunno, Tosh,' said Owen quietly, 'but I'd watch the coffee for a bit.'

Ianto grinned as he walked away. Coffee? Oh he had a better imagination than that… And they knew it. And would be thinking about it all the time. Everything they ate or drank. Every bit of equipment he got for them. Everything. Oh the next few days were going to be fun.

Even without Jack.

FIVE

Jack was looking up Wharf Street. Again. What was this, the fourteenth time, the third this century?

Not much had changed.

At times over the years, the odd house had become squats for students (especially popular during the late 1970s and early 1980s), but they never stayed long. A few bums would sometimes try to find shelter there, but they too would disappear back to the cold streets of Butetown or Grangetown rather than stick in Tretarri.

Towards the end of the 1990s (a period Jack remembered far too clearly), much of Cardiff Bay began to be done up, ready for the Millennium – gentrified was the usual term. The old buildings had been torn down or converted into luxury waterside apartments. Businesses moved in, tourist holiday spots shot up and, directly above the Hub, a massive complex of shops and restaurants was created.

But half a mile away was Tretarri, untouched, like a film set or a living museum for the past.

Although nothing seemed to live there for long.

Jack noticed a piece of yellow paper tied to a lamp-post and went to read it. Encased in rain-protecting plastic, it announced a proposal by Cardiff Council to redevelop Tretarri, make it full of expensive homes with no car parking, like the rest of Cardiff.

Good. It needed someone to finally force the life back into it.

Maybe, after all these years, whatever caused Jack to stay out of the streets, whatever made him feel ill, would go away. Maybe he'd buy a flat there, just to spite whatever it was.

He dug into his pocket and pulled out a Torchwood PDA, calibrated by Toshiko to detect Rift activity.

He'd assumed decades ago that Tretarri had to be a real Rift hotspot but, each time he'd tried to take readings, no luck. This was Toshiko's work though – she was damned good at this kind of thing.

He raised the PDA and stepped forward, already feeling the nausea rising in his stomach, but determined to get as close as possible to try and achieve some kind of reading.

Of course, he could've brought Gwen or Ianto with him. But that would have meant revealing this little chink in his armour – admitting that there was something unsubstantiated, unreal, untouchable that hurt Captain Jack Harkness. Jack was cool about such things normally but, after all these years, he'd come to think of this collection of roads and houses as his thing, his pet project. Something he needed to do by himself.

The PDA blinked at him. Yes, Rift energy was present around Tretarri, but no more so than, say, up by the new shopping complex behind The Hayes, or down by the football ground at Ninian Park. In other words, Tretarri offered nothing extraordinary, no explanations as to why he couldn't get past whatever this invisible barrier was.

'Damn.'

He shoved the PDA back into his voluminous coat pocket, took a deep breath, closed his eyes and walked forward. Each time he tried this trick, wondering if it was a barrier that would disappear if he couldn't see his surroundings (he'd encountered artificial barriers like that before).

Nope, two steps in, he was ready to retch. Four, and the bile was already in his throat.

He opened his eyes and turned around, facing directly away from Tretarri.

And found himself facing Ianto and the SUV, a folder of paperwork tucked under his folded arms.

'Evening Jack,' he said simply, lifting the folder. '1912,' he recited. 'Agent Harkness was observed in Tretarri, touching the air. Has he lost his mind? 1922: Jack Harkness seen "entertaining" a young lady at the edge of Wharf Street. When she ran to one of the houses, he became agitated until she returned. They engaged in sexual deviancy in the back of the Torchwood Daimler he had previously requisitioned. 1979: Jacko – "Jacko", really? – anyway, Jacko and a guy with a Mohican, throwing things into Bute Terrace, breaking windows. Is this the kind of behaviour the Torchwood Institute should tolerate?' He tucked the file back under his arm. 'Irregular, Jack, I'll give you that, but regularly irregular enough to pique my curiosity.'

Jack shrugged. 'You read too many files, Ianto. It's not good for you. You'll strain your eyes.'

'You knew you'd get found out eventually. Better me than Owen or someone else after we're all dead and forgotten.'

'Oh, you're in a cheery mood tonight. Weren't we going on a date at some point? No offices, no roofs, right?'

Ianto ignored that. 'And what happens, Jack, when one day you take the requisite four-day holiday noted in these files but never come back because whatever it is you're doing here decides it's had enough of you getting nowhere and takes action?'

'Are you challenging me? You? Honestly? I think I preferred the old "wouldn't say boo to a goose, forever calling me *sir*" version of Ianto Jones.'

'You disappeared on us once before Jack.'

'Yeah, and you got a holiday in Tibet out of it. Stop complaining.'

'You know what I mean. Four days. Does it always take you that time to recover, or do you come here four days in a row?'

'What do the files tell you?' Jack grinned at Ianto, that grin that always worked.

Ianto just shrugged. 'I'd rather you told me.'

Jack stared at his friend. Confidante. Team mate. Lover? Well…

He sighed and pointed behind him. 'This place. For nearly a century now, I've been trying to walk around it, go down a street, knock on a door. Something. Anything. But no, I can't get past… whatever is stopping me. One thing that file won't tell you is why I get ill, because I don't know.'

Ianto walked past Jack and into Wharf Street, easily as anything. He turned back to Jack and threw his arms wide. 'Nothing strange here, Jack.'

Jack frowned. He was sure the street lighting had grown fractionally brighter while Ianto was speaking. And there was a light in one of the nearby windows. That hadn't happened before.

'Come back to me, Ianto. Slowly.'

The Welshman did as he was told, but Jack wasn't watching him. Just as Ianto drew level with him, the lighting noticeably faded. Jack nodded to himself.

'Did you see that?'

'What?'

Clearly not. 'Never mind. I'm thinking this is all just in my head. After all, there's nothing dangerous here. Call this Jack's Pet Project and forget about it, yeah?'

'And are you still taking your time off?'

Jack considered – maybe one day it would be time to find some answers, helped by the one thing he'd not had before. A team of friends he could rely on. Who would do as asked without a stream (well, there'd be a trickle, of course) of mad questions he couldn't answer.

But not yet. He needed to get to the bottom of this by himself, Jack decided. Then grinned at Ianto. 'Yeah. A few days. See you round.'

Extract from diaries left to the Museum by Michael Cathcart in 2004

October 1954. Friday. Sad news, they found that old tramp Tommy and his dog dead in the street last night. Just down off Coburg Street, linking Wharf Street with Bute Terrace. Shame, he was a good'un at heart. Always telling tall stories about the history of Cardiff. Never got to the bottom of the thing with the lights he was talking about a few months back that I wrote about in Journal 17. Nice dog, too. Only been with Tommy a couple of years.

Headstone in St Mary's Church, Llantrisent

Here lies the body of Gideon ap Tarri 1813–1881

Now in the arms of God

Reunited with Marjorie, taken 1876

Obituaries, **Western Mail**, *14 July 1986*

Morgan, Silas: Beloved father and husband. Accidentally taken from us during the Tretarri fire.

Western Mail, *13 July 1975*

RETURN OF THE TRETARRI GHOSTS

Local police were out in force last week to clear a group of "squatters" from Wharf Street. The group of mostly teenaged males claimed that they were happy to leave as the house they had "adopted" was "haunted". "There's ghosts and spooks in there, man," said 19-year-old student Bryan Mathews.

Rumours of ghosts and other supernatural events have been reported in the area for several years. Local priest Reverend Allan Smith of St Paul's, Grangetown, whose parish the Tretarri area falls under, was dismissive of the reports. "While there are indeed many things in this heaven and Earth for which we have no explanation, I don't believe that spirits of the dead are living in Tretarri."

Extract from **Mid Glamorgan Morning Star**, *26 June 1986*

Disaster struck as the Fire Crew responded to the fire in Hanover Street, Tretarri Estate at around 4 a.m. yesterday. A tree in the front garden of the Victorian terraces collapsed in flames in front of the fire engine, killing the driver and one of the firemen instantly. A third foreman was pronounced dead on arrival at St Helen's Hospital. None of the victims have been named.

Extract from student newspaper **The Heath, 6 August 1978**

... as mentioned in the reports a couple of years back on the guys kicked out by the "authorities" from Tretarri. But it's important to remember that what they said they saw has never been followed up, never been explained and now Tretarri is derelict again, denying us potential student accommodation. We contacted the Housing Officers at City Hall but, of course, they wouldn't comment. As that Pistols guy says, "Never trust a hippy"...

Extract from diaries left to the Museum by Michael Cathcart in 2004

May 1947. Tuesday. Went to Tretarri, see what all the fuss was about. But nothing. No ghosts, no ghouls, no visitations of any kind. Just a tramp, old Tommy, who's been living in and around Grangetown for years.

Extract from memos between L Morris, BBC H of RF (London) to R de Houghton, BBC Ctrllr L P – docs. 01.02.1961

Sir – as noted in our memo of Monday last, we have checked and rechecked the tapes. Everything that was recorded in Cardiff is blank. However, as my producer explained to Asst Ctrllr L P – docs and features on Thursday, we had done some editing work, so I know the damage to the tapes occurred after we returned to BH, for we listened to everything through before making an editing script for the Pas to work from.

Extract from Building Commission, 3rd quarter 2005

… trees lining the street need to be cut right back. Planning permission refused for change of use from house to three flats at 38 Gainsborough Gardens. Planning permission pending for conversion of attic space at 116 Riley Road, Canton to bedroom and en suite WC. Planning permission granted for demolition of entirety of Tretarri estate, work to begin by September, construction of new apartments and office space to be put out to tender by 3 November. Planning permission refused for 69 Prospect Avenue, Ely for construction of two garage spaces in rear garden…

Extract from Local History pamphlet, on sale in Wales Millennium Centre shop, 2007

The area referred to as Tretarri was established as a small town in 1872 by Gideon ap Tarri, landowner of West Grangetown and North Penarth arable land.

Extract from diaries left to the Museum by Michael Cathcart in 2004

January 1961. Saturday. Tretarri is becoming a legend apparently. The BBC were there, a Light Programme about ghosts the man said. I offered to show them my journals, my diaries, but they weren't interested. Bloody English, so ******** superior.

Obituaries, Western Mail, 14 July 1986

Sheppard, Martin: Devoted husband to Helen. Accidentally taken from us during the Tretarri fire.

Extract from Fire Examiner's report (suppressed under Govt Resolution 8A/dcl/1913)

My people could find no evidence of fire damage to any of the terraced houses in Hanover Street, Coburg Street or Windsor Street. Eyewitnesses, including the surviving firemen, all reported identical descriptions, within reason, of the fire and the gutting of at least two of the houses, on the corner of Coburg Street and Bute Terrace, formerly occupied by illegal immigrants from Albania. This inexplicable event is exacerbated by the occupants all receiving invitations to a restaurant in Butetown that night for a family birthday celebration. The Albanians all reported, when interviewed separately, in different police stations within Cardiff, that the restaurant did not exist.

Government inspectors accessed the area but reported feelings of paranoia, of trepidation or general fear and mistrust when they explored the neighbourhood.

Extract from Cardiff Bay and Its History *by Eleri Vaughan (TaffTours Ltd, 1992)*

The legends surrounding the area known as Tretarri are as fanciful as the area itself. Too small to be a real town or village, Tretarri is little more than a cluster of Victorian streets built as a vanity project by mine owner Gideon Tarry, who adopted Cardiff as his hometown in 1852, after changing his surname from his birth name, Haworth.

His claims to be a Welshman were finally disproved ten years ago by students at Cardiff Grammar, researching biographies of famous Welshmen for a modern Domesday Book. Tarry's origins and subsequent death remain clouded in mystery but it is known that he invested a great deal of money building Tretarri, ostensibly for workers. However, no workers ever lived there after 1876 – the 'town' itself is seen as an eccentric form of the traditional Victorian Folly beloved of so many rich landowners during the late nineteenth century.

Obituaries, Western Mail, 14 July 1986

Brennon, Bruce Peter: Widower. Accidentally taken from us during the Tretarri fire.

Extract from Fortean Times, issue # 867

… amongst the weirdest bodysnatching rumours is that of Gideon Tarry in Wales, England. This bizarre reclusive landowner disappeared from the city of Cardiff in or around 1881. Some years later, a grave was located in a North Cardiff churchyard he never frequented as it was quite some way from his adopted home in Penarth. A frequent subject of gossip during the twentieth century, Tarry's body was exhumed twice – the second time because of what occurred the first time. Reports state that the headstone was taken down during the excavation to discover if money, jewellery, etc were secreted in the coffin with Tarry's body. The headstone was broken in two accidentally and put inside the church vestry for safekeeping. The coffin itself revealed no treasures, or indeed anything else – because there was no coffin, no matter how far down they dug. A day later, investigators returned to find the ground replaced and looking untouched, and the headstone seamlessly repaired and resituated. The ground was consecrated once more and after a lengthy legal battle, the headstone was removed and the grave freshly dug eight years later, using more sophisticated equipment to find where the coffin was. No coffin was found and once again, the ground was re-laid, the stone reset by persons unknown.

Obituaries, Glamorgan Voice, *21 May 1856*

Haworth, Tarri: Master craftsman and respected businessman, of Penarth. A swift and shocking sailboat accident took this beloved husband and devoted father, aged 63. Funeral at St Teilo's Church, Wednesday week. All welcome, including working classes to whom he holds a special place in their hearts.

Extract from Building Commission, 1st quarter 20??

Reversal of 2005 submission and subsequent approval. Application to restore Tretarri without any substantial building work and no demolition to occur. Uplighters to be placed in the pavements, new street lighting to be installed and each forefront of the houses to be cleaned and restored. Trees to be trimmed back. The ground floors of 1 and 3 Coburg Street to be redeveloped as a retail unit. No other houses are to be entered, or interfered with in any way. Approved by Cardiff Council.

[NB: Date of issue and proposer and seconder illegible]

SIX

With a sigh, a really quite loud, one might almost say melodramatic sigh, Ianto closed the last file on the screen, and picked up the buff folder containing pre-electronic age sheets of paper. It had two Torchwood logos on it, the modern hexagonal one and a sketchier version, which, experience told him, meant this particular file was started around the 1920s.

'Problem?'

Owen was coming up the small stairway from the Autopsy Room. Ianto thought that Owen was spending too long down there in the cold, sterile atmosphere. Since giving up his desk on the upper level to Gwen, he'd buried himself down with the tables and cold storage trays. It couldn't be healthy.

That said, Owen smiled more these days. Perhaps being away from the watchful eye of Jack made him more cheerful. Or perhaps he was even weirder than Ianto had previously thought.

Ianto held up the folder of real paper items. 'Everything is incomplete, out of order and a mess. The online files aren't much better.'

Owen didn't take his eye off his PDA and whatever readings he was inputting, but he did pause before carrying on. 'Well, you know what, I blame whoever is in charge of keeping everything up to date and efficiently ordered. Now. Who would that be?' And he then looked up and grinned that slightly lopsided grin he had. 'Oh, wait. That's you, isn't it?'

He was heading towards the back of the Weapons Room, to the steps that took him up to the walkway level and the Hothouse. After clattering up the steps, he paused before pulling open the Hothouse door and entering the world of bizarre alien botanics inside.

'You need to stop worrying, mate. If Jack's not fussed about Trewotsit, why are you?'

Ianto opened his mouth to reply, and realised he didn't have an answer. Was it because it was about Jack? Was it because he didn't like mysteries? Perhaps it was simply that, having started the research and found it a bit of a mess, his dedication to perfection – or anal retentiveness, depending on who you asked (oh, he was aware of what the others said about him) – was drawing him into the strangeness that was Tretarri.

By the time he was ready to admit that he didn't actually know, Owen was shut away with the plants, spraying a couple of them with a small nozzled water-gun, and occasionally reading off from his PDA.

With a shrug to himself, Ianto returned to the files. And was immediately disturbed by the huge cog-shaped doorway rolling aside to reveal a giggling Gwen and Toshiko as they scuttled in, carrying a couple of pizza boxes each.

'Hiya,' Gwen called sweetly. 'What's your poison tonight?'

Ianto looked at the pizzas and shook his head. 'Oh. No, thank you. No. No pizza. For me. You carry on. Enjoy.'

Gwen looked strangely at him. 'You OK?'

Ianto nodded. 'Sorry, just distracted. And not hungry.'

She and Toshiko were out of his eyeline now, obscured by the base of the water tower sculpture that housed the Rift Manipulator.

He'd worked with Gwen for a year or more now, but something about her still made him slightly flustered, like he felt he was being judged and so was always trying to impress her. Which was daft, but he couldn't stop it. Jack had noticed it; he'd made some joke about Ianto's schooldays and asked whether he'd had a crush on a teacher.

Stupidly, Ianto had started to tell him about Miss Thomas – and Jack hadn't let him forget it.

He needed to say something normal to Gwen.

'So, how's the wedding? Rhys all right? Found a hotel yet for the reception?'

Gwen's frowning face popped back into view. 'Fine. Great and, umm, no not yet. Oh, know any good DJs?'

'My mate Paul,' Ianto said. 'But you probably wouldn't want his kind of music. A bit... cheesy...'

Now it was Toshiko's turn to pop her head round. 'Cheese pop? It's very in apparently.'

'No,' Gwen said. 'I think Rhys's best man knows someone. So long as he doesn't play "Agadoo", I'll be happy.' There was a pause, then Gwen suddenly spoke seriously. 'Ianto, have you spoken to Jack? What's with these days off? He's not crashed out here, as far as I can tell.'

Ianto instinctively looked towards Jack's office, where Jack spent his nights down in a small bunker. Where, frankly, there wasn't room for two, whatever Jack said.

'Hasn't he? Oh. Well, I imagine he's found a hotel or something.'

'We wondered,' Toshiko threw in, 'if he was at your place?'

'No,' said Ianto, a fraction too quickly. 'No, why would he be at mine? What's at mine that Jack would want? I mean he could be anywhere, why my place?'

'Blimey,' said Owen from behind and above. 'Someone's a bit jumpy about jolly Jack Aitch tonight.'

Ianto looked up and saw Owen, a plant in one hand, water-gun in the other. And hoped he hadn't gone red. 'Anyway,' he continued, trying to cover his overreaction, 'we need to look into all this stuff. There's something about Tretarri that is… off.'

'"Off"?' queried Owen.

'As in "not good"?' Gwen asked, as Toshiko fired up her screens.

Ianto joined them at their workstations, as they both started looking stuff up, Toshiko obviously a bit faster at creating a database to filter the words 'Tretarri', 'Gideon Tarry' and 'Gideon ap Tarri'.

Twenty minutes later, Ianto had told them all he knew. The four of them were down in the Boardroom, staring at the big screen, and Toshiko was giving one of her lectures.

'As Ianto realised, Tretarri has been the focus of a lot of weird and wonderful happenings. Mysterious fires. People trying to live there but unable to stay for reasons they couldn't explain. Even animals go a bit doo-lally if they enter the area.'

'"Doo-lally"?' asked Owen munching on chilling pizza. 'Not another new technical term?'

'I quite like "Doo-lally",' said Ianto, which got a smile from Toshiko.

'Oh well, if suit-boy likes it, we'll adopt it as Torchwood's new motto. "Everything's a bit Doo-lally".'

'People,' admonished Gwen. 'Back on the subject at hand, yeah?'

Owen smiled at Toshiko. 'Sorry, Tosh. I gather we're back in the sixth form.'

Toshiko then outlined the current plans the Council had to refurbish Tretarri. 'This will result in two things, at a guess. I stress "guess" – we don't actually know.'

'We don't actually know why we're doing this in the first place,' Owen said. 'I mean, it's not as if we even know this is Rift-related.'

'It's Jack-related,' Ianto said quietly.

There was a pause, then Owen looked at Toshiko. 'Guess Number One, nothing happens and a crappy bit of Cardiff gets a facelift. Guess Number Two, all hell breaks loose as contractors etc go doo-lally as they try and work there. Right?'

'Spot on.' Toshiko smiled.

Gwen looked at the guys. 'Ianto, can you research a bit more, find out about this Gideon Tarry person, see if there's anything in his past we need to be aware of.'

'Like he's a Rift Alien in disguise?'

'That kind of thing. Owen? I want you to plough through the medical records of people connected with Tretarri with me, find out if there's anything we can extrapolate today that they couldn't ten, twenty or fifty years ago, yeah?'

'Yes ma'am.' Owen gave a mock salute. 'I'm also keen to work out what it is that knocks Jack for six, but no one else.'

'Good. Tosh? Can you take your portable Rift Detector Thingy—'

'More technobabble,' laughed Owen. 'Love it.'

Gwen silenced him with a look. 'As I was saying before something annoying buzzed in my ear, can you see if you can get into Tretarri and locate anything Rifty?'

'I walked in easily enough,' Ianto stated. 'But not for long enough to notice anything. Although…'

'Yes?'

'Nothing I can put my finger on. But Jack… I think Jack saw something when I went in. But he never said what.'

Owen shrugged. 'Is the plan to get this wrapped up before Jack comes back?'

Gwen nodded. 'So, Ianto?'

'Few days left I reckon, if I understand the files. It seems to take him never less than four days in total to recover.'

'Hey kids,' said a voice behind them. 'What's going on?'

The others looked at Jack framed in the doorway, grinning and clearly full of fitness and health. And, as one, they turned and stared at Ianto. They were not pleased.

An hour later, they were still in the Boardroom, with the addition of coffees all around.

'I have noticed,' Owen said quietly, 'that when it's just us, no coffee.'

'Jack arrives,' agreed Toshiko, 'and oh, look, the coffee gets made.'

'Delivered,' Gwen added, 'by hand.'

Ianto just shrugged. 'I like Jack. The rest of you? I can take you or leave you.'

And he grinned wolfishly at them.

Toshiko suddenly remembered the teasing a couple of days before. She looked at her coffee in alarm. 'Ianto, you didn't…?'

'Didn't what?'

'Nothing.'

Ianto smiled inwardly. Gotcha. Paranoid about coffee.

With Jack now at the head of the table, Gwen brought him up to speed.

'Really guys,' he said, 'you don't have to do this.' He placed his PDA on the table and slid it over to Toshiko. 'Although, by all means sift through this. It's what I recorded at the site.'

Toshiko scooped the PDA up. 'Jack, I think we all want to sort this. Not just for you but we're all scared Ianto will poison us if we don't.'

'Slowly,' added Owen.

'In the coffee,' Gwen clarified at Jack's quizzical frown. 'Teamwork,' she finished.

Jack shot a look to Ianto, who just smiled back, stretched his arms, then rested his head on his hands.

'OK,' said Jack. 'Sometimes the humour still passes me by.'

'Who's joking?' muttered Ianto. He smiled around the table, then stood up and started clearing the coffee mugs away. 'Collecting evidence,' he whispered to Owen as he passed behind him.

Jack looked at Gwen. 'I want Owen to run tests on me, get to the bottom of my problem. Then Tosh should go look at the site and—'

Gwen held up a hand. 'Got it covered, Jack. All sorted. Teams briefed and ready to go.'

Owen and Toshiko wandered out. Ianto made to follow them, but hung back just long enough to hear Jack and Gwen.

'You enjoy taking charge, don't you?' said Jack, not unkindly.

Gwen just said what they all thought. 'You left us once Jack. God knows you could do it again. Now this – someone has to be ready to step up and get the job done when you're somewhere else. Still your team, Jack, but never underestimate us. Let the bad guys do that.'

As she left the room, Jack looked at Ianto. 'I never underestimate anyone on this team. Do they really think that I do?'

Ianto gave a shrug. He hated this conversation. Permutations of it had arisen a few times recently. 'Couldn't say, Jack,' he just said. 'But I don't think it's a reflection on you, just something you've instilled in them. Not a bad thing.'

Jack stared at him a moment longer. 'Been a long time since I wasn't the last voice on things around here. Takes some getting used to.'

Ianto slammed the tray of coffee cups down, making Jack jump.

'Damn it, Jack – it's not like that. They'd follow you into fire if you told them to. But you're not the most predictable man in the world. If they are going to die for you, for Torchwood, give them enough credit to make their own decisions about where, when and why they're doing it.'

Ianto took a deep breath, picked the tray up again and looked Jack straight in the eye. 'If you don't mind my saying so.'

SEVEN

Toshiko stood at the corner of Bute Terrace, her PDA discreetly hidden under a newspaper she had bought.

She had no idea what the paper was, or what any of the headlines were. Whatever the news was today, she had most likely heard about it ten hours previously, as the Torchwood computers sifted every line of communication across the globe, flagging up anything interesting. Exactly who decided what was interesting, Toshiko had never quite understood – although she and Jack had modified the Hub's computer systems together over the years, neither of them was entirely sure where it had come from in the first place, whether it was set up in Cardiff or had been something imported from London or somewhere else. Jack remembered, he told her, that one day when he'd visited the place it wasn't there, the next it was. But this was at a point when he wasn't regularly working for the Institute, so it could've been added at any time between those points. As systems went, it was probably the best in the world.

Jack had told her once that UNIT had enquired if they could borrow her to upgrade their systems, but he'd fobbed them off. She knew that Jack Harkness wanted Toshiko Sato's expertise for himself. And she was more than content with that. She and UNIT weren't exactly… mates.

So here she was, trying to take better readings than the ones Jack had got from the streets, since she was able to venture inside. Which was intriguing in itself.

She and Owen had spent most of the previous night in the Hub, thrashing Jack's problem through. She enjoyed spending time with Owen on problems. They worked well together, nights in front of computer screens, or alien artefacts, munching on sandwiches – they occasionally used to have hot food until Toshiko one day managed to… Well, now she just referred to it as 'the toaster incident'. A phrase which always seemed to amuse Owen far more than it ought to.

Of course, there were times when it was difficult. Times when she wanted to just lean across the desk, times she wanted to tell him that she—

Anyway, that was irrelevant. Not conducive to a good working relationship. People at work shouldn't—

Mind you, there was definitely something between Jack and Ianto. And that was a work situation. And—

But no. No, not Owen. He'd never understand. They'd talked once about how, in their line of work, it'd be really difficult to find someone who could ever really understand them, and Owen had said that girls like that were so rare they were extinct.

Toshiko had wanted to grab him and scream and yell at him and point out 'I'm right here, you stupid—'

Even if she had, Owen still wouldn't have got it. He'd have made a joke about it, deflected it with his unique brand of humour. Because God forbid that Dr Owen Harper should ever realise that what he was looking for was right under his bloody nose if only he wasn't so damn arrogant and convinced he was right, and if he'd just kiss her and hold her and look into her eyes and—

Jesus!

The horn was incredibly loud, and Toshiko felt her heart actually jump as it thundered in her ears. Still surprised, she turned round and realised she was in the path of a huge Council truck that was coming to begin the gentrification of Tretarri.

A man in a hard hat and suit walked over.

'Can I help you?' he asked, his name badge announcing him to be Ifan Daffydd, Scheme Manager.

She knew all the details of the redevelopment work, having hacked into a number of public and a few very private records about the redevelopment. This meant that she could now shove her hands into her mackintosh pocket and produce an extremely accurate facsimile of a Council pass, giving her full authority to observe, enquire and generally stick her nose into any and all aspects of contracted work going on today and over the next few weeks.

'Toshiko Sato, from the Senedd. Checking up on architecture, historical importance, blue plaques for famous Cardiff comedians, actors or raconteurs. That sort of thing.' She showed her pass.

He offered a hand and she shook it. Firm, dry, casual. Good, not hiding anything then.

She pointed at the truck. 'Took me by surprise, sorry. I was daydreaming.'

Daffydd shrugged. 'Not a problem. How can I help?'

'Talk me through what's going on.'

'Well,' Daffydd said, leading her to the pavement, 'the first thing we're doing is putting in this revolutionary new lighting. It's wireless, like one of those Internet routers. We put a box on here, and then embed in the pavement a series of halogen bulbs, protected by shock-proof glass. These will be arranged to a specific pattern and at a series of convex angles, and apparently, on a winter night, the beams should hit the underside of clouds and create a series of patterns. The lights have a series of gels that can be activated, creating different coloured patterns too.'

'Colour me impressed,' Toshiko laughed.

Encouraged by her enthusiasm (faked, but he didn't know that), Daffydd took her to one of the plasterers' trucks.

'Then these guys will go into the houses, most of which we're converting into luxury apartments, and we will be putting in similar wireless devices to control the electricity supply. Can't do it with the gas pipes, sadly, but hopefully these places have a degree of safe gas and water piping – we'll be checking all that. But basically our intention is to disturb as little of the structural integrity as possible.' He pulled a brochure from his inside pocket. 'These are some of the colour schemes and a 3D CG illustration of the streets, lit and with new trees planted. In twenty-four hours, this place will be a beacon for Cardiff's redevelopment schemes.'

Toshiko was about to nod her approval when something occurred to her. 'One day? To do… everything?'

'Yeah, it's great isn't it? These guys came highly recommended by the company who developed the electrical routers. Part of their service. Council buys a few hundred, each router services ten houses, we get 'em delivered and fitted for free along with the whole refurbishment job.'

Toshiko smiled, hoping that her PDA's encoder was recording the conversation. 'Must cost a packet,' she said.

'Dunno,' Daffydd replied, moving closer and leaning forward conspiratorially. 'But you know, I don't think so. City Hall seemed very keen, so it can't cost more than the traditional way, and it's quicker and makes less carbon footprints. Apparently.' He paused for a second. 'Never been quite sure how they work all that carbon footprint stuff out myself. I reckon none of them do, it's just PR jargon.'

Toshiko moved towards him to reply. And to let the PDA do its stuff and get a good reading of Daffydd, in case he was an alien. 'You know what, Ifan. I think you're right. It's all just hot air for the electorate.'

She shook his hand again, gripping it tightly, hoping he didn't think it was a come-on. 'Pleasure to meet you. I'd best leave you alone and get back to the Bay. Tell everyone you're not knocking down any local treasures. Thank you.'

Daffydd smiled and turned away.

'Oh, Ifan,' Toshiko called to him. 'Do you know who actually designed all this refurbishment? The architect, I mean. We have no records at the Senedd, it's all still in Crickhowell House or up at City Hall, and I was just wondering…'

Daffydd threw over the pamphlet. 'Keep it. Architect is on the back.'

Toshiko turned it over and stared.

There were the architect's details: phone number, email, address and a long list of local Welsh (and a couple of Glaswegian) projects he had overseen.

And a photo.

'Oh my God…'

'Oh, I don't think so, Ms Sato,' said a smooth-as-silk voice behind her. 'I think you'll find real gods are few and far between these days in Cardiff. You and your… associates saw to that.'

She swung round, knowing who would be standing there.

Sure enough, mid-70s, in his immaculate pinstripe suit and cravat, slicked-back silver hair, wide eyes bursting with intellect and… malevolence.

Just as he had looked the last time she saw him.

Just as he had in the architect's photo in her hand. She glanced down at that once more. 'It can't be you,' she murmured.

And so Toshiko never saw the punch which knocked her out cold.

EIGHT

Rhys Williams was at a table in the café at the end of the arcade, looking over at the new shopping development nearing completion opposite.

Apparently, Cardiff needed more shops.

He noticed that no one seemed to have considered that lorries would have a hard time getting down the slim roadways. Oh well, perhaps they'd sort that out later.

Things you think about when you run a fleet of delivery trucks.

He glanced at his watch and at the cold coffee opposite him. Every time they arranged to meet, he'd buy Gwen a coffee in the vain hope that it would somehow magically cause her to turn up at the agreed time. It never worked.

But he didn't mind. They were getting married soon. She had said yes. YES! To marrying him! How bloody brilliant was that!

'Daf, she said yes!' he'd said triumphantly to one of his drinking buddies the day after.

'Hey, Banana, how's Lanzarote? I got some news, mate,' he'd said to another on the phone.

'Mam, it's Rhys. I got some news for you. Great news. Well, I think it's great news. Well, it's great for me. No, I told you, I won't know about the job for a couple of weeks. No… no, will you listen… Look, you better sit down then… No, I've not had an accident, Jesus, will you let me speak?' That one had gone a bit downhill, truth be told.

And today, he and Gwen were going to agree on a venue. Well, he suspected he was going to be told what the venue was. And who was coming. And what he was wearing.

And you know what, that was fine. Because he was marrying the most fantastic woman in the world and, so long as she had the wedding she wanted, that was good enough for him!

So long as bloody Torchwood didn't get in the way – oh God, maybe that's why she was late. Maybe Jack bloody Harkness, aka God, had told her she couldn't have the day off.

Did Torchwood even do days off?

He never asked her that. Somehow the idea of Handsome Jack signing leave forms appealed to Rhys.

'Excuse me, it's Rhys Williams isn't it?'

Rhys looked up at the old guy stood beside him. Smart dresser, bit… you know, *fey*, his mam would say. Maybe it was the voice.

'Umm, yeah?'

'You look well. Better than the last time I saw you.'

'Have we met?'

'You might say that. Once upon a time, in a different life.' The old man produced a business card.

Rhys read the name and shrugged. 'Sorry mate…'

'That's quite all right. I'm… a friend of Gwen's. I gather congratulations are in order.'

Rhys grinned. 'Thanks very much.'

The old man grinned too. 'I just wanted to say how nice it is to meet you properly, and I hope you have a long, happy life.' And the smile was gone. 'Because the price paid for you to have this one was terribly high.'

And Rhys felt a bit awkward. Was this guy a loony? Did he really know Gwen?

Oh, he could ask her, there she was.

'God Rhys, I'm really, really sorry,' she said, coming through the door and heading to the seat.

Rhys turned to present the old man, but he was gone.

'That's odd,' he muttered. 'There was a scary man here, wanted to say hi.'

'Who was he?'

'I dunno. Knew me though. And you. Said he was a mate of yours.'

Gwen looked around the crowd in the café, looking for someone she knew.

'He said some strange things,' Rhys finished. 'Oh, and he left you his card.'

Gwen took the card and Rhys saw the colour drain from her face.

'You OK, love?'

For a moment, all Gwen could see, all she could imagine,

was Rhys's bloodied corpse stretched out in Torchwood's Autopsy Room. All she could remember was Bilis Manger taking Rhys from her. It would not happen again.

When she spoke, Gwen's voice had lost all warmth, all humour. Instead she was cold. Colder than he'd ever heard her. 'Rhys. Go home. No, no stay here. Stay out all day. Go to the pub. Call Daf, have him get pissed with you, but on no account go anywhere alone. You need a piss, Daf goes with you.'

'Now hold on—'

And Gwen's hand was on his, squeezing so hard she was almost crushing it. 'Please. Trust me. Never be alone till I call you. Even if that means you don't go home or go to work or do anything for a week.'

'This is—'

'Don't say "bloody Torchwood", Rhys. Seriously. This is big. I can't explain, trust me.'

And Gwen turned the card over and read something Rhys hadn't seen, written in neat, precise handwriting on the back.

Next time, it said.

Next time there'll be nothing you can do, 'Widow' Williams.

NINE

City Hall was an impressive array of buildings and, no matter how often Jack Harkness stood outside them, he couldn't help but be impressed.

Coat flapping in the breeze, blue shirt, red braces, navy chinos, Jack was an imposing and strikingly attractive figure.

At least, that's what he hoped the man he had come to visit would think. Still. It'd been a while. They'd not parted on the best of terms last time. Little things: Torchwood policy, words about trust and betrayal, antiques and a cold spaghetti bolognaise that had been slaved over for a good fifteen minutes led to bitter recriminations, name-calling and a bloody good bitch slap, of which Jack was the recipient.

Thinking about it, Jack touched his left cheek. It had been a good slap, and not what he'd've expected from someone so... unimposing.

Still, appearances could be deceptive. Wasn't that what

they said on Earth in this era? Oh, if they only knew the half of it.

He entered the building and, avoiding the tourist routes to the marble hall or the conference rooms, he nudged open an insignificant door to the right, which led to a concrete stairwell, peeling paint and dust on each step. No one regularly used the stairway, which is why Jack always liked it. A fast in and out.

But then, that was Jack through and through.

He kept going until he reached the fourth floor and eased open the doorway into a plushly carpeted hallway, a series of doors on either side, with a huge ornate one at the far end. Outside it was a small desk, and sat at that desk was a small, thin blond man in a suit and tie, probably half a size too big for him.

He had stunning blue eyes, and Jack briefly flirted with the idea of sneaking up on him and snogging him.

The man was reading a sheaf of notes and tapping with one hand on a PC keyboard.

Jack realised sneaking up wasn't going to work. Not in the corridor. Shame.

'I saw you come in, Jack,' the young Welshman said. 'And no one but you would use those stairs.' He still hadn't looked up.

'Oh. Right. OK,' said Jack. 'How are you? It's been a couple of years.'

'It's been twenty-two months, eight days and about nine hours, Jack. Lots of things could've happened to me in twenty-two months, eight days and about nine hours.

Nice of you to ask now.'

Jack stood still. He still wasn't being looked at. Boy, some people could hold a grudge.

'Slapped anyone recently?'

The man dropped the notes onto his desk and finally gazed straight at Jack.

'Oh, tried to feed anyone an amnesia pill in cold pasta recently?'

Ouch. Yup. Grudge time.

'Oh come on, Idris. You gonna let that little… incident come between us?'

Idris Hopper stood up. He wasn't as tall as Jack, but the Torchwood leader took a step back anyway – Idris was not happy to see Jack, that was clear.

'You screwed with my head, Jack. On so many levels. You lied, you cheated. You betrayed me, my trust in you. And then you tried to poison me.'

'It wasn't poison. Don't be so melodramatic. It was for your safety.'

Idris said nothing for a moment, then he strode past Jack and opened an office door.

'Jan, I need to pop out for a few minutes. Can you keep an eye on the Mayor's desk for me? Ta love. I'll get you a donut.'

He then turned back, grabbed Jack's arm and, with strength that belied his slight stature, almost dragged Jack back to the stairwell.

He slammed the door open and shoved Jack into the vestibule. Jack hit the wall with some force, turned to yell at Idris, and discovered the young secretary snogging him. Hard and ferociously.

After a few seconds, Idris pulled back, his eyes full of anything but love.

'There, you got what you wanted, Jack. Happy now? Will you finally leave me alone and get the hell out of my life?'

Jack was speechless at first, then ran a hand through Idris's hair. The younger guy pulled further back.

'Don't touch me, Jack. You don't have that right.'

'I'm sorry,' Jack said. 'I didn't realise it'd affect you that much. How long did it take for the pill to wear off?'

'I thought the point was that it wouldn't wear off. That people you dosed up stayed amnesiac for good, those memories scratched out of their lives?'

Jack nodded. 'But occasionally a shock or just a strong personality can overcome it. Depends on the strength of the pill I used on you.'

'And you don't remember, do you? I bet you never remember any of the lives you screw around with at Torchwood, do you?'

Idris went past Jack and down the stairs. 'I can't have this conversation here. Outside. Now.'

Jack paused. 'You know, I'm not usually one for following orders, Idris.' He shrugged. 'But I do kinda need your help.'

Jack followed Idris down and out of the building and across the grass. They crossed the road at the traffic lights and walked silently into Cathays Park, just behind Cardiff's famous castle.

For a few moments, neither of them said anything. Then Idris sighed. 'Well?'

'Well what?'

'Well what do you actually want today, Jack?' Idris checked his watch. 'You have five minutes. Real minutes, not Torchwood minutes.'

'Like I said, I need your help. I need records.'

Idris laughed humourlessly. 'That was what you said last time, after Margaret Blaine disappeared. Remember that? My boss, the Mayor. One minute you and your mates are chasing her, the next, she's gone. Death by Earthquake was the official answer.'

Jack looked hard at Idris and remembered the confused young man he'd seen at the bus stop one day, a bundle of books under his arm.

The man who'd run over, shouting 'You! It was you!'

Jack had had no idea who he was.

'I saw you, at the office!'

Jack turned and headed back down, past the Millennium Centre and towards the water tower. He hadn't banked on Idris's determination and, when he stepped onto the special stone at the foot of the tower, the stone that was part perception filter, Jack should have effectively vanished. Not in a blink, but in a peripheral vision way; Idris should have believed he'd just lost sight of him for a second.

But as Jack stood there, using his Vortex Manipulator to activate the elevator at his feet, Idris was still facing him, still shouting straight at him.

'Yes, you! The American!'

And Jack realised Idris could still see him. Which was unfortunate as the elevator began its descent.

Idris was open-mouthed. The last thing Jack saw before he sank below pavement level was Idris screeching 'Bastard!'

As the elevator reached the Hub, Jack stepped off, yelling for Toshiko.

'Guy by the tower, staring at our so-called invisible elevator.'

'Got him on CCTV,' Toshiko replied. 'What about him?'

'I need to know who he is. He knows me, I haven't set eyes on him before. And I'm pretty sure I'd remember a cute Welsh blond, blue-eyed geek like that.'

'Geek chic your thing, is it now?' asked Suzie Costello, Jack's number two.

'Jack has "things"?' Owen called out from his workstation, next to Toshiko's. 'I thought Jack just shagged... anything.'

Jack ignored them and headed to his office. Something tingled in his mind.

He began flicking through Suzie's reports: sightings of a Gladmaron Cruiser over Pontypool; a Weevil cluster in a ruined church; some aliens wanting to serve a writ on Earth for transmitting offensive radio waves at their star system (Toshiko had worked out from the time-distance ratio that they were getting broadcasts of Hancock's Half Hour from the late 1950s); no sign of Torchwood Four still...

His door eased open and Suzie came in, putting a printout in front of him. A CCTV image of Idris, and his ID pass from City Hall.

'Personal Assistant to the Mayor,' Jack read. 'Nope, why me?'

'The Mayor, Jack? She disappeared a month ago – after the earthquake.'

And Jack remembered.

'You insisted we all stayed down here, all four of us. No one was allowed to go outside the Hub till it finished, cos you said you knew it'd be OK. Remember?'

He nodded. 'Good job, too. The earthquake could've damaged this place more than the last couple did.'

Suzie shrugged. 'You keep too many secrets from us, Jack. Teamwork, yeah?'

Jack smiled. 'I'll deal with Mr Hopper,' he said and waved a bottle of amnesia pills at Suzie.

She shrugged and went back out to talk to the other two.

Jack thought about how he'd had to stay down below a month before. Because there was another him up above, 150 years younger but identical to look at. There'd not only been the risk of confronting himself; if Toshiko, Suzie or Owen had seen his earlier self, he'd have had to explain his past to them. He adored them, yeah, but that was a step too far.

He knew he'd have to deal with poor Idris now. He took a level two pill out of the box – twenty-four hours would be enough to have Idris forget seeing him without causing too many problems for him at work.

Now, how to get it to him.

That new Italian restaurant, on the corner of Mermaid Quay, by the fish and chip place (he'd never understand twenty-first-century humans and the allure of fish and chips).

He left the office, grabbed his greatcoat and went back to the elevator.

'Using the lift wise, Jack?' asked Suzie.

'Nope,' he replied. 'But it'll get his attention.'

Which it did.

Jack stood there, facing Idris. 'Idris Hopper, no one else but you can see me. Quite an achievement on your part. Well done you. Fancy a drink?'

Idris said nothing, just looked at the passers-by who were ignoring Jack completely, although one woman gave Idris a very peculiar look.

Jack stepped off the stone and a teenager instinctively swerved round him, muttering a 'sorry' as if it were perfectly normal.

As they walked to the Italian, they chatted about Idris (he was single), his family (his mother was dead, his father had moved to Newport six years ago), the movies he watched (he utterly hated the movie version of Hi Fidelity and had seen Finding Nemo a few more times than might be considered healthy) and his hobbies (he loved rare and antiquarian books, spending most of his less-than-stellar salary on them, and restoring some of them, which he'd then sell on at book fairs and suchlike). Once they'd sat down and ordered, Jack explained Torchwood. And perception filters. And aliens. And the missing Mayor. And the aliens that came through the Rift.

Three hours later, Idris was agog, untouched spag bol on a plate in front of him, utterly convinced by Jack and his explanations.

'You know, Idris, Torchwood could use a guy like you in a position of authority. Keep an eye out at City Hall for weird happenings, let me know. I'd really like you to be our point man, a sort of affiliated agent.'

'I can't, I work for the Council,' Idris said. 'I mean, they take precedence.'

82

'Oh sure, of course,' Jack said. 'No one would ask you to betray the office. No, it's just more if we get something, and we think we could do with a gap filled in, maybe I could call you and you help me. And of course, if it'd break confidences from the new Mayor, then I utterly understand, yeah?'

Idris wanted to think about it and excused himself. As a waiter went by, Jack asked for Idris's food to be put in a microwave for thirty seconds.

'We don't use microwaves here, sir,' said the snooty guy.

So Jack put the pill in Idris's food, burying it in the sauce. Making sure no one was looking, he aimed his Manipulator at it and gave it a tiny burst of energy. Not enough to hurt Idris, but it'd certainly warm the food up.

When Idris returned, they finally ate.

'You live locally?' Jack asked.

'Century Wharf,' Idris replied.

'Nice. Gonna make me a coffee?' Jack smiled.

And now, here he was, smiling at the memory in Cathays Park.

This time, Idris wasn't smiling. 'You're thinking about that night, aren't you? When you poisoned me. Or whatever.' Then Idris gasped. 'My God, for the first time I just realised. I could've had sex with you that night – that's what you wanted. And if your pill had worked, I'd never have known.'

'Oh I think no pill is strong enough to completely erase the memory of me in bed,' Jack laughed. Then stopped.

Idris wasn't laughing.

'So, add moral corruption to the list of Jackisms, yeah?'

Jack shrugged. 'Nothing happened. God, did nothing happen. I wasn't used to being turned down, you know.'

'And just like your perception filter not working on me, nor did the pill.'

'One in 80,000, Tosh reckoned. Completely immune.'

'So tell me, Jack. What happens when aliens raid the supermarket? And you drug everyone, but someone like me doesn't get the effect. And they remember everything. Do they turn up a week later, face down in the Bay? Or wake up in hospital a vegetable? Or get swallowed by an earthquake?'

Jack had no answer. Because, yes, once that had been the Torchwood way. That was a Standing Order from Torchwood One in London. But things had changed, and Jack had broken direct contact with London. And thrown their rulebook away. Since then, the problem hadn't arisen.

'I'd like to think that, like you, I could convince them to help us. For the greater good. But the situation hasn't arisen. And the amnesia pill hads been revamped since then anyway. It's closer to one in 800,000 now. Better odds all round.' Jack grinned.

Idris stood up. 'So, what do you want? And don't say "another kiss" because no, not now, not ever.'

Jack threw his hands up in protestation. 'Furthest thing from my mind,' he lied, convincingly he hoped. 'I need information. And not just PR-level stuff, but deep stuff. The who, why, how and did I say why?'

'About?' Idris checked his watch. 'Thirty seconds, and I'm gone.'

'Tretarri.'

'The redevelopment? Why?'

'How involved do you want to be, Idris?'

Idris looked at him. 'You got a USB reader on you?'

Jack produced his PDA.

'Nice,' said Idris. 'I'll be back in ten. If I'm not, it means I've changed my mind and I never want to see you or anyone else from Torchwood ever again. Is that clear?'

'As crystal.'

And Idris headed back to City Hall.

Jack wasn't sure if it was worth waiting. But then, he was a pretty good judge of character – and Idris was, at heart, a good guy, with a Jack-sized chip on his shoulder.

Jack stared at the people milling around the park. And again, that feeling of pride in humanity hit him. So much wrong with the planet, so much wrong with their lives if only they realised, and yet nothing would stop them. As a people and as individuals, calamity might hit, but they always found a way to bounce back. Twenty-first-century humans were great.

And somewhere was an ancestor of his. Walking around, unaware that one of the descendents from a colony world 3,000 years into the future was sat in Cathays Park, Cardiff. At least he hoped they were unaware.

Assuming he was descended from humans. Hmm… A bit of family tree research might be in order. If he ever got the chance to go home, which he was in no hurry to do.

'Excuse me, Captain Harkness?'

Jack looked up. A young brunette, early twenties, was standing in front of him. She smiled and passed him a USB flash drive.

'Idris asked me to give you this. And something else, which he said I'd have no trouble giving you.' She smiled. 'And he was dead right.'

And she snogged him, passionately. Hard, long and very probingly.

After a good minute, she slowly drew back, and ran a finger across his lips.

'Wow,' she breathed, then turned and walked away.

'Wow indeed,' Jack said quietly. 'God I love these people.'

He watched her retreating figure, slim, tight ass, nice legs… and blew air out of his cheeks, then got his PDA out and inserted the flash drive into it.

Info copied across and he read it quickly. Details of the redevelopment, plans, conveyancy reports, recommendations for construction crews, requisitions for trucks, concrete, trees.

Details of a fast-tracked licence for food, drink, music and street performers for a week-long party, stipulating no sale of alcohol in case of minors.

And the architectural plans.

It all seemed innocuous enough, but he'd get Gwen and Ianto to plough through it, check dates and so on. There had to be something.

Idly he opened a few reports. Nothing on the surface.

He was about to give in for a bit, when he clicked on the architects' plans.

And saw the architect.

He considered going straight back to Idris, but decided his time would be better spent back at the Hub. Instead he sent Idris an email via his PDA.

Thanks for the information. So, this guy doing the architectural design. He intrigues me. Tell me whatever you can about Mr Bilis Manger x

There was one house in Coburg Street that no one went near. No one really knew why, some put it down to the general feeling about Tretarri, but no one stayed long enough to work out why.

It wasn't true, all the newspaper reports, the ones that said no one ever lived in Tretarri. We did. Group of us on Bute Terrace. Number 9. We were on the corner of Coburg Street, and number 6 was the weird house.

Michele and Janet had done some research on the area. During the war, people had tried hiding here to escape the Cardiff Blitz, but had ended up taking their chances on the streets of Butetown. Martin found out by going through the local papers that as far back as the thirties the place was rumoured to be haunted. I mean, people would turn up here, move in, settle, whatever. Then inexplicable events occurred, lights, phantasms they often called them, noises. Dogs and cats died, fresh food went off, light bulbs would die then come back to life, brighter than before and objects would move around the place.

Michele and I woke up one morning to find our bed had moved across the room in the night. We assumed Janet or Marty had done it while we were asleep, but Marty hadn't come home that night, and no way could Janet have done it by herself.

There were a few other student houses in Tretarri, but people didn't stay long – and we realised after a few weeks, one house wasn't occupied at all. I mean, never. We looked into the windows, I swear it hadn't been touched since it was built, no sign of anything modern.

Marty talked to some old guy who'd lived on the streets for years in the area, and he was chatty – especially if there was a few pounds and some chocolate in it for him. He said he'd seen people come and go from every home, but not number 6.

Because it was haunted. He said it was haunted by the lights. We weren't sure what he meant because he also said there was a man in the house too. Who lived there sometimes, but he'd never seen him. We didn't understand that. He said no one ever saw him, but they knew he was there.

So we all decided to break into number 6 and spend the night there, like... like a ghostwatch, I think.

We took a camcorder and a cassette deck too as back-up. Marty suggested a ouija board, but I thought that was a bit... stupid

(Interruption by DI Laurence, asking if Mr Garrett considered a ouija board to be dangerous.)

No, I mean, it's just a bit of crap really, all that "mediums" and "Doris Stokes" stuff. But Janet, she was scared I think, so I put my foot down. Said no.

So anyway, that night, we got in. I don't know who actually got us in, I was a bit late cos I'd had to check the camera out of the student union, so the other three were there with sleeping bags and beer and stuff by the time I arrived. I set up the camcorder by the door, so it took in the whole of the, well, living room I s'pose. It meant we were on camera all the time.

I turned it on around eleven, when Michele went out to get the Chinese, and I'd stocked up on 90-minute tapes, so it meant one of us had to wake up every so often to change tapes. So we sorted out a rota. I said I'd stay up first, till the first tape ran out. Michele would do the next and so on.

I sat up while they slept, changed the first tape but was still wide awake so let

Michele sleep on. I had a book for class to get through, which was fine. I changed the second tape about two and thought I'd wake Michele up.

But I must've dropped off cos the next thing I knew, Marty and Michele were giggling to each other, and it was about four thirty.

And he had the bloody ouija board and was moving the glass around with his fingers. God knows what Michele thought Marty was doing, it was so obvious he was spelling I AM A GHOST or whatever but she thought it was funny.

I watched them for a few minutes and hoped Janet wouldn't wake up or she'd freak.

Then I noticed the camera wasn't recording, so I whispered to them but they ignored me.

So I got up. And that's when they looked at me. Straight at me.

And that was… that was when it must've happened. God, it must've been then, and I didn't understand.

I didn't notice their eyes at first, I saw the smiles. I can see the smiles now, I mean, not really smiles, something so cruel, so twisted… Then I saw the white eyes. Not just white, but like, like bright lights, I'm telling you, it was freaky. I thought maybe something was reflecting into their eyes, cos I couldn't see pupils or anything, just white… light I s'pose. But there was nothing else on, nothing to reflect.

Janet woke up, I know that cos I heard her swear and yell at them about the Ouija board.

And that's when I was really scared. Yeah

scared, cos they ignored us both then and went
back to the board, and I'm telling you, mate,
that glass was moving by itself.

And it spelt out two words, I dunno what they
meant. Torch and Wood. I thought it meant they
were going to burn the building down.

And I can still hear Michele now speaking but
it wasn't... I mean... it just wasn't her voice,
you know? Someone... something else spoke, I
dunno, through her? Hold on, let me think about
this. Can I have something to drink please?

(Tape stops, then resumes, DI Laurence re-
identifies everyone on the tape and states the
time and date. See separate report for exact
timings.)

OK, thanks. Yeah I'm OK. Right. So, the voice.
Janet is well freaked now, and I'll be honest,
mate, I'd almost wet myself. That voice.
So cold, it felt like we were in a freezer
suddenly. An abattoir or something.

And Janet and I staring at them, our mates...
and Michele spoke to us but it made no sense.
She just said about the darkness and Phyllis
and the lights. It made no sense. And Janet
and me, we ran, I mean just got the hell out
of there. But we tried to get to the front
door and that's when we saw the ghost. I saw
the ghost. Janet says she's not sure what she
saw, but I'm telling you, it was a bloody
ghost. A bloke, sort of there and not there.
I'm not talking the whole white sheet, Scooby-

Doo thing, but a bloke stood there. I could see he was speaking, shouting almost, but couldn't hear anything he said.

And we were out of there.

But this is important because I think, yeah, yeah, I'm sure sitting here now, I think it was saying what Michele had been saying – the mouth, I'm picturing it, "darkness" and "the lights", I'm sure that's what it was yelling.

And then you lot turned up the next day at uni and arrested me. But I'm telling you, that's what happened. We didn't hurt them or anything. Why would I kill Michele – we were together, if you know what I mean. I wouldn't do that to her.

Where's Janet – she must be able to tell you this... I mean, she was at uni too, wasn't she? You must've got her when you got me, she'll tell you they were... They weren't dead when we ran... ran away... from them...

TEN

Ianto closed the file and added it to the pile on Jack's desk, just as Owen sauntered in.

'Just us chickens, yeah?'

Ianto nodded. 'Looks like it. We sit around at home while the womenfolk go out and do all the work.'

Owen grinned wolfishly. 'Don't let Jack hear you call him a woman!'

Ianto managed a smile back.

Owen nodded at the files. 'Heavy going?'

'Yeah. And nothing concrete in any of them. Just read about some poor kid whose two mates, were found immolated in number 6 Coburg Street. One of them was his girlfriend. The police tried to pin it on him and another girl, but there wasn't enough evidence. Poor kid said it was the ghost.'

'Once upon a time,' Owen said, sitting on the edge of Jack's desk, 'dunno 'bout you, mate, but I'd've laughed at that. But in our world, ghosts and all that, who's to say what is and isn't real?'

Ianto shrugged. 'S'posed to find out, aren't we? But I'm not seeing anything that links the Tretarri area with Jack's weirdness. You got anything?'

'Nah, same old test results you always get from Jack – normal for him, less normal for us, but at least he's consistent.'

Ianto pondered on this. 'Look, I found out he's been doing this for... years. I mean with back-from-the-dead Jack, how many years is open to interpretation, but well over seventy-five. So it's not something new. And we know he's not always been based at Torchwood, although he's been in and out of here for a long time. So whatever it is that stops him going in, it's before Torchwood. It's something in him.'

'Ask him,' Owen suggested. 'Seriously. Say it's time for some answers.'

Ianto thought about this, too. 'I'd like to offer him some options, cos you know him – he'll just clam up, brush it aside. But if we can piece some stuff together from what we do know, we could challenge him.'

'You can challenge him,' Owen corrected. 'I'll just get my head bitten off.'

'Maybe you will. So what do we know?'

'Bugger all, frankly. I sit down and try and put two and two together where he's concerned and always get five.'

Ianto was enthusiastic now. 'Exactly, and maybe that's the way to get answers from Jack. We draw wrong conclusions, hopefully he'll correct us.'

'Or let us believe 'em, cos it suits him that way.' Owen pulled up a chair and sat down. 'Right. He's old. Dead old. Been here since Queen Vic was on the throne, Tosh reckons. And he can't die, which – and I say this as the best doctor studying alien biology in the world – I can offer no grounds for. His cells just go back to how they were. I've studied his blood, tried messing around with it. It doesn't reform, it doesn't mutate or even clone itself. It just reverts back to how it was before. Which, frankly, is bloody weird and not a bit scary.'

'Time Agent. When we met Captain John, he said they were Time Agents.'

'Never told us what that meant though. But hang on… What if, assuming this isn't all bollocks and they're not conmen doing the most protracted swindle in history, what if they can travel in time. That's gotta do something to you, I'd've thought.'

'How do you mean?'

Owen frowned. 'The human body, it's designed for certain stresses, certain events in your life. But is it designed for time travel? I'm not saying it isn't, but we don't know it is. We do know that Jack's the only person actually unable to enter Tretarri, even if no one else stays for long.'

'And,' Ianto worked it out slowly but surely, 'Jack is the only time traveller we have to hand.'

'So maybe that's the connection. Whatever makes him able to stand time travel, makes him unable to get into Tretarri.'

'Which would,' said Jack from the doorway, 'mean that

whatever is in Tretarri, is related to chronon energy of some sort.'

Owen had his hand on his chest. 'One day, Jack, one day, you'll give me a heart attack, sneaking up on people like that.'

Jack smiled, and put his hands on Owen's shoulders, to keep him in the chair. 'Nah, physician, heal thyself.' He looked at Ianto. 'OK, I like the theory, how about I give you some interesting evidence. Ianto, any names come up in your files and records that should raise our collective eyebrows?'

Ianto frowned. 'Dunno what you mean.'

'Try this name for size—'

'Bilis Manger,' shouted Gwen as she crossed the Hub to join them.

'Hell, is everyone out to get me into A&E today?' Owen asked.

'Phyllis!'

They all looked at Ianto.

'It wasn't *Phyllis*, it was *Bilis*!' Ianto threw the file about Owain Garrett to Jack. 'Read that.'

'Where's Tosh?' Gwen asked.

'What? Who the hell is Phyllis?'

'Phyllis isn't Phyllis, she's Bilis!'

'Hello? Tosh? Remember her?'

'Heart rate still really fast.'

'Bilis is a cross-dresser?'

'No, he thought the ghost said "Phyllis" but I bet it said "Bilis"!'

98

'Toshiko Sato?'

'Ghost?'

'We have a transvestite ghost?'

'It's in the report.'

'Idris told me it was Bilis. It's all on this flash drive.'

'Who the hell is Idris?'

'One of Jack's floozies, from, oh, just before you joined, I seem to remember.'

'Small? Japanese? Good with alien tech?'

'Is Idris a cross-dresser, too?'

'What?'

The Hub lights went out en masse.

'Emergency procedures,' yelled Jack.

'Lockdown? We have thirty seconds or we're here for six hours if it's a complete power cut!'

'Shit! My samples of Jack's blood and DNA – I need to keep the power to them going!'

The lights came on again.

Gwen was standing at her workstation. 'Next time I turn them off for good,' she snapped.

'Why did you do that, Gwen?' asked Owen as they all left Jack's office.

'To get you lot to shut the hell up. Now then, I'll ask again. Where is Tosh?'

'Dunno.'

'At Tretarri, I think.'

'She hasn't called in though.'

Gwen was about to say something to all this when a new voice called out.

All four Torchwood heads turned and looked past the base of the water tower and up at the raised Hothouse.

Tosh was there, unconscious on the grating. Beside her, hands behind his back, cool as a cucumber, was Bilis Manger.

'Good evening,' he smirked.

The click was almost deafening as four guns – three Torchwood pistols and Jack's Webley – were drawn, aimed and cocked in unison.

Bilis just smiled more. 'Oh really, surely you know by now that you don't get rid of me that easily. You may all be very fine shots, but I'm not sure you'd actually open fire and risk hitting Ms Sato when faced by a harmless and desperately unarmed old man.'

'Harmless,' sneered Owen.

'We don't know you're unarmed,' Ianto pointed out.

'Not convinced you're as old as you seem,' Gwen added.

'But I'll give you "desperate".' Jack smiled, lowering his gun. The others followed suit.

'Oh Jack, Jack, Jack. Poor, sweet, time-lost Jack. How you wound me with your cynicism. Such ingratitude when I've gone to all this trouble. For you.' Bilis looked at Gwen. 'How nice to see you again, Gwen. And I'm so glad to see your Rhys is looking better these days. And Owen Harper. No, wait, *Dr* Owen Harper – one must subscribe to the social niceties. I really wanted to thank you. After all, it was down to you that my Lord was able to escape his shackles. And Ianto Jones, without whom nothing would ever really get done at Torchwood these days.'

'What do you want?' spat Jack. 'Kinda bored of you now.'

'Simple Jack. You destroyed Abaddon. You closed the Rift. It reversed time, repaired all the so-called damage that was done. And so I am left wondering: if all those people out there came back to life, like dear Rhys, what happened to my Lord?'

'It was destroyed,' Jack said quietly. 'I destroyed it. That was what closed the Rift, sealed the breach. He's not coming back.'

'Ah,' Bilis said, still smiling, 'you would say that, wouldn't you?' He gestured to the Rift Manipulator housed in the base of the water tower. 'This marvellous device, this wonderful creation affects the Rift itself. Who is to say that someone with experience of manipulating time couldn't find a way to go back a bit further? To take my Lord out of harm's way?'

'Me actually,' said Jack. 'I don't know if you can do that, but I doubt it. A lot. But even if I didn't doubt it as much as I do, you're not going to get the chance to try.'

Bilis nodded. 'I imagined that that would be your response. Hence my borrowing of your technical genius here. Oh, you don't mind if I hang on to her, just for a little while longer?'

'Know what? I do,' said Jack. 'Funny little thing, loyalty, but she's part of my team. And I rather like her, too. So work needs plus friendship needs equals me not really willing to part with her.'

'Trade?'

'Offer?'

'I'll exchange Toshiko for a day in your Hub, access all areas, and I promise not to let the Weevils out.'

Four stony faces greeted that request.

'Well, it was worth a try,' Bilis said. 'Au revoir.'

Before anyone could react, Bilis and Toshiko had vanished again.

'Damn,' said Owen.

'Gwen,' snapped Jack. 'Records, now. I want any trace of Bilis found. Start with this.' He threw the USB flash drive to her. 'I want to know everything there is to know, and extrapolate the rest.'

He looked at Owen. 'If your hypothesis about me is correct, I'm useless in Tretarri unless you can find a way to overcome it.'

'Gotcha,' said Owen disappearing down into the Autopsy Room.

'Ianto. You, my office. I want to know everything you've gleaned about Tretarri from your research. I'll be back in five.'

'Jack?'

Captain Jack Harkness turned back to Gwen and smiled. 'I'll get her back safe and sound, Gwen. I promise.'

Gwen held his look for ten seconds, and smiled.

'I know you will.'

ELEVEN

The Vaults had been the cornerstone of Torchwood for ever. They represented the good and the bad side of everything Torchwood stood for, both modern Torchwood and the Institute set up by Queen Victoria nearly 130 years earlier.

Bilis Manger stood on the sensible side of the glass that formed the cell door.

Within, the Weevil stared up at him from the floor, mewling slightly in fear.

Bilis tapped on the transparent, if somewhat stained, strengthened plastic. 'I wonder what use I could make of you, my friend.'

'Not a lot, I'd guess,' said Jack from the main doorway. 'I knew you'd be here. Revisiting the scene of your last crime. The murder of Rhys Williams.'

'You took longer getting down here than I expected, Jack.' Bilis smiled, without looking away from the Weevil. 'I may call you Jack, I assume. It's just that they all do, so it seems sensible.' He paused for a beat, then continued. 'I was going to ask if you ever used your own name any longer. Or indeed, if you even recalled it.'

Jack said nothing, but his hand edged closer to his holstered Webley.

'Oh, do stop relying on your toys,' Bilis said. 'We both know you can't hurt me.' He pointed at the Weevil. 'How long have they been on Earth, then?'

'No one really knows,' Jack replied. 'The Torchwood Archives are… curiously vague.'

'Almost as if someone has gone through them, I imagine, erasing odd bits of information.' He smiled again. 'Archivists are a funny sort. So dedicated to their work, their accuracy, yet not above the odd bit of subterfuge when necessary to protect… whatever they've individually chosen to protect. That's the joy of life, Jack. To protect what we love. Remember love?'

Jack shrugged. 'I remember you did everything you could for a demon from God knows where that almost destroyed Earth. Was that out of love?'

'Love. Passion. Belief. Duty. The lines blur sometimes. There are over fifteen recognised major religions on this planet. One religion believes something different from another, and yet so often it's just the same thing with a different name, or a different form of worship, or a different headdress. But they will fight to protect what they believe in, no matter the cost. You've been here a while Jack. How many wars, how many lives squandered on religion? On belief? On that blurred line between love, duty and belief. Then we get to science. Science versus creationism for instance. Two opposing stances on the same subject, neither of which has any real evidence to back it up. What a bizarre time you washed up in.' Bilis finally looked at Jack. 'Happy here? You used to have so much more… freedom.'

'You know so much about me. I know so little about you.'

Bilis turned back to the Weevil. He placed his hand on the transparent plastic and the Weevil echoed the action from within the cell. 'What do you know about the Weevils? Only what you research. You're exactly the same as that Weevil to me, Jack Harkness. A savage beast, worthy of investigation, nothing more.'

'What do you want?'

'I'm on a mission. Redemption. Atonement perhaps. A way to show those who matter that I can make up for my errors, and the tremendous pain you cost me.'

'What do you need from me? If it's about me—'

'Oh yes, it's certainly about you.'

'Then why involve Tosh?'

'Ms Sato is personally… immaterial. She's just the clichéd hostage. It might have been Gwen, or young Ianto. But I'll tell you one thing, Jack, I wouldn't have wasted my time with Owen.'

'He'd have fought back, you mean.'

Bilis shook his head sadly, looking down at his feet now.

And Jack saw, lying there, a gun. A pistol. Not a Torchwood-issue one, just an average revolver. It was smoking from the barrel, as if it had recently been fired.

'No, he just isn't worth it.'

Jack looked back down, but the gun had gone.

Bilis looked at him, and Jack realised the vision of the gun seemed to have surprised Bilis as much as it had him. 'Some things are beyond our control. Yes, even yours and mine, Jack.'

'So, where's Tosh?'

'Safe in Tretarri for now. Number 6 Coburg Street.' He ran his finger around the cravat he wore, loosening it fractionally. 'Ask Ianto. He'll get the reference if he's as good in the Archives as he should be by now. By the way, he's picked up Torchwood's history very quickly. I'm impressed. You should be, too.'

Jack said nothing, just kept watching.

'So, what is all this about? You still need an answer, don't you? Even though I have told you.'

'OK, so you're pissed at me over Abaddon. Big deal. You set a ninety-foot demonic "great devourer" on the streets of Cardiff, Torchwood take it down. That's life. Deal with it.'

Bilis swung round, and Jack took an involuntary step back. For the first time, Bilis's face was twisted in anger, in hate. And something else, something Jack couldn't quite identify. Fear? Panic? Anguish?

'Revenge, Jack. Revenge for the future!'

Before Jack could speak, a hoarse voice behind him gasped out.

'Jack. Help me!'

And crouched down by the door was someone Jack hadn't seen in over sixty-five years.

'Greg? Greg Bishop?'

'Sorry, Jack – not strong enough… Can't fight the light. Can't fight Bilis. Or the darkness. Can't help you any more…'

And Greg was gone.

Jack touched the bare Vault wall where he'd been, both a second ago and in 1941.

'I'm sorry, Greg,' he said.

He straightened up and turned back towards the cell, but he was not surprised to see Bilis had gone.

Stuck to the Weevil's transparent door with a piece of sticky tape was a note in red ink.

No. Not ink. Blood.

REVENGE FOR THE FUTURE.

TWELVE

When Toshiko woke up, she found herself lying on a cold, hard floor. She gently sniffed the air – nothing distinctive, but not airless. No chemicals, so not anywhere industrial. No damp, nothing stale.

She slowly opened her eyes.

The first thing she saw was a chair. A basic wooden seat, like at a desk. Oh yeah, and that thing there, that was a desk. OK. Not immediately threatening.

'Hello Ms Sato,' said a voice.

There was someone sat in the chair, she could see the legs. Male. Suit.

Oh God, it was Bilis Manger, wasn't it?

Hang on – he'd hit her or something.

'Stop pretending, Ms Sato. You have been fully conscious for five minutes and… wait… thirty seconds.'

She rose slowly, keeping an eye on Bilis, who had his back to her.

He didn't seem particularly threatening. But then, he was

just an old man who could travel in time, walk through walls, disappear into thin air and, oh yeah, tried to destroy the world with his precious devil-thing.

No threat there, then.

He held out an arm and clicked his fingers. Almost instantly, as if someone had switched on loud music, Toshiko heard clocks ticking.

As if previously they'd been on pause…

'Where am I, Bilis?'

He turned and looked at her, resting an arm on the back of the chair, to all intents and purposes regarding her as a schoolteacher would a mildly intelligent pupil that had passed a test.

Kind of patronising.

He smiled. 'Welcome back. I do apologise for needing to… temporally disable you, but it was important.'

'I felt nothing,' Toshiko said, trying to be as emotionless at possible. 'So you didn't even hurt me.'

Bilis shrugged. 'I wouldn't waste time hurting you, Toshiko. If I'd wanted to do that, I could just as easily have killed you. That would have been neater.' He turned back to his desk. 'I need you. For now. If you'll excuse the pun.'

Toshiko couldn't see the pun, so she ignored it. Instead, she tried to get her bearings. Instinctively she tapped her ear.

'You are a little out of range,' Bilis said, again somehow knowing what she was doing. 'You've done it thirty times so far,' he added. 'I've viewed every permutation of every action. Such is my curse.'

110

'Curse?'

'I see time, Toshiko.' He sighed. 'I made a deal once, and I am still paying the price. I can cross into history, and into possible futures. Not far into the future obviously, that would be catastrophic, but I see enough.' He stood still, with his back to her, then reached his arms out. 'Everything.'

Toshiko was in a shop, she realised that now. A Stitch in Time, she remembered Gwen saying it was called. Timepieces repaired and restored. Or stolen in the past and brought to the present to be sold as antiques.

'How far back can you go?'

'I don't know. I do know, however, that it would be foolish to go back too far. Every action has an opposite reaction. I learned that to my cost a long time ago.' Arms still outstretched, he finally turned to face her.

His eyes were gone – in their place were tiny orbs of burning white light, tendrils flickering around the lids and the bridge of his nose.

'Right now,' he continued, 'we're in that tiny splinter between now and then, next and last, here and here. And this is where I met them. And they gave me a task, something to do while I grieved for my Lord, who you took from me.'

Toshiko was getting lost. 'Why did you knock me out? What did you do when I was unconscious?'

And Bilis smiled a horrible, cruel smile. 'As I said, I needed to disable you temporally. I fear you misunderstood. I meant exactly that. You are outside time as you know it, Toshiko Sato, because I have a task for you.'

'Which is?'

He grabbed her hands so she couldn't wriggle free. 'Let me show you your true potential.'

And Toshiko was somewhere else, watching someone else, seeing through someone else's eyes.

It was a street in Cardiff. A building she didn't recognise, brand new. All concrete and blue-tinted glass.

A car pulled up, a small sports car – Toshiko wasn't an expert on cars, but she could recognise something smart, new and expensive. The doors opened automatically, upwards. The passenger got out, briefcase, smart jacket and skirt, hair swept back. Power-dressed to the nines. On the briefcase was stencilled a logo in leather; she recognised it as a slightly modified Torchwood logo.

Oh my God, somehow, she knew, this was the new Hub, but right at the heart of the city centre, in full view of everybody.

Staff were gathering on the steps, applauding lightly and uniformly.

The woman from the car looked up, adjusted her glasses, smiled at the assembled staff and then placed the case on the floor and returned the applause.

It was Toshiko.

After a minute, the car driver joined her. Sharp suit, similar glasses. Owen Harper.

There was something wrong though – it was his hand, his left hand. It was metal and, as it flexed, she could hear dozens of tiny servos moving the fingers, and she just knew this was some kind of alien prosthetic, linked into his nervous system, working perfectly in unison with the rest of his body.

Owen took Toshiko's hand in his, and she now noticed the weddings bands.

Toshiko and Owen, married?

She and Owen!?!

Toshiko Harper spoke to quieten the applause. 'People, thank you. You've done us all proud. Today, this building stands as a testament to the work of Torchwood throughout the Empire. Five years ago, Torchwood was buried away, ashamed of its roots, ashamed of its past. But today, we stand proud, we stand tall and, above all, we stand united with all the other Torchwoods across the globe, throughout the entire Empire.

'I am honoured to be your CEO. Mr Harper here, Owen, is, as you know, going to head up our science and medical divisions. Mr Lawson there – good morning Eric – will run logistics and Mrs Williams, who sends her apologies, but the baby just wouldn't wait and she went into labour last night—'

There was another round of applause.

'—and she's using Torchwood tech to ensure smooth delivery and a healthy baby boy should be here in about, oh, three hours. Anyway, when she returns to work, Mrs Williams will head up our humanities division. Welcome, ladies, gentlemen and others—'

At this, a small grey alien pushed through the crowd and stood at the front, applauding lightly.

'—Everyone, welcome to Torchwood Cardiff. The home, the heart and the soul of the Torchwood Empire. We run planet

Earth, ladies and gentlemen, let's treat it and its peoples with the love, care and dedication that they deserve.'

More applause.

Toshiko turned to Owen. 'You think he would approve?'

Owen laughed, squeezing his wife's hand. 'Nah, he would've hated all this, but you know what, deep down, I think he'd be proud of what you've achieved in his name.'

'And let's face it, lover,' Toshiko replied, 'without his unique properties, none of this would have been possible. You could say he's still the heart and soul of the Torchwood Empire.'

They passed the crowd, nodding at various staff, shaking hands with a couple of divisional leaders. Two great glass doors slid open, and the flock of people followed their leaders in.

The atrium of Torchwood Cardiff revealed forty storeys of offices, labs and R&D areas. Below, an undisclosed number of basements, sub-basements, vaults and state-of-the-art cells, containment areas and other secrets.

In the centre of the atrium, next to the reception desks, was the old water tower, moved from its original home in the Bay, now stretching up towards the high ceiling, the Rift Manipulator on display to the world at large.

And at the foot of that was a glass rectangle embedded in the floor.

Inside was a figure, wired up to something hidden beneath the rest of the cream-coloured concrete flooring, tendrils snaking away from every joint, every inch almost of the body, powering… powering Torchwood itself.

No wonder they said he was the heart and soul – the body was Captain Jack Harkness, trapped in a frozen moment of time, his immortality being drained and, in turn, running the entire Torchwood Empire.

Toshiko looked down into the glass container, Owen smiling that thin, almost cruel smile of his, at her shoulder, always one reverential step behind his wife and mistress.

'And as for you... what can I say?' Toshiko was asking. 'You showed me the truth, you showed me how anything could be achieved if I just explored my potential.'

'No greater responsibility than potential,' Owen added. 'You told us that.'

And Toshiko leaned in and touched the glass. 'I owe you everything.'

'Oh and Jack?' This was Owen. 'Thanks again for this.' Owen flexed the artificial fingers on his left hand. 'Best birthday present ever.'

Suddenly, there was a commotion at the door, two guards went flying and a tramp ran in. No, not a tramp, but a dishevelled young man, screaming obscenities in Welsh, shoving his way through the crowd.

'He's got a gun,' screamed a young woman, somewhere.

Sure enough, a pistol was in his hand, and he waved it around, as if focusing, looking for something specific.

Or someone.

'You!'

He was looking for Toshiko and Owen.

Twenty large, armed guards surrounded the CEO and her escorts instantly.

Owen eased himself through the crowd. 'Ianto, mate,' he started to say, but the ranting Ianto cut across him.

'I want him back! Now!'

'Not possible, mate,' smiled Owen. And he pointed at the glass slab beneath his feet.

Toshiko waved the guards back as Ianto stepped forward and saw Jack's contorted, agonised body.

Then, faster than should have been possible, Ianto raised his gun and fired twice, the first bullet straight through Owen's forehead. As the corpse fell, the second bullet hit Toshiko's shoulder.

Thirty guards opened fire, and what remained of Ianto Jones would have needed tweezers to collect together.

Toshiko had a hand pressed against her bleeding shoulder as she knelt next to Owen.

She looked up at the guards. 'Get him to my suite – now.' Then she turned to the bloody mess that was spread around where Ianto had stood.

'Welcome to Torchwood, Ianto,' she muttered. 'Jack would've been proud.'

And the real Toshiko, the one watching this awful, terrifying vision of her future, shivered as her vision swam, bright lights popping in her vision until everything was blotted out by a white haze.

Then she was back to herself, standing in Bilis Manger's strange shop, holding his hands, and staring into his face, his eyes still gone, still replaced by that same blazing white light. The lights bled from his eyes and roared into hers. Toshiko ceased struggling after three seconds as her body filled with the white light.

And Bilis's own eyes returned to normal.

'And now you have a share of a stronger, younger host,' he murmured.

Toshiko stood there. Why couldn't she move? Why couldn't she see properly? Why was everything so bright...

And then she realised, as consciousness began to fade again, that the light was inside her. Not in Bilis.

The last thing she was aware of was the touch of his hands on hers. 'I'm sorry,' he said quietly. 'I'll make sure nothing bad happens to your body. Well, nothing too bad. That's the best we can hope for. When we make deals with the Light and the Dark.'

THIRTEEN

'Jack,' Gwen called as he emerged from the basement, 'there's nothing after 1941.' She waved towards her monitor. 'Same newspaper reports as last time about the dance hall, then nothing. Bilis Manger simply vanishes.'

'What about that wretched shop he had?'

'Gone,' called Ianto, from Toshiko's station. 'No records with the Council, it was never there. It's been a clothes shop since 1998. Paid up, account in the name of Julia Martin, who seems to be a model citizen of Wales, bar a few speeding fines and a hefty overdraft.'

Jack frowned and passed a sheet of clear plastic sheeting to Gwen. 'Scan it, it has Bilis's handprint on it. Silly idiot put his hand on a cell door. I want every system in the world checked, Scotland Yard, Interpol, the FBI, CIA, Mossad, the works. Someone must have encountered him, someone else must have some info.'

'UNIT?'

'Been there, tried that, called in a favour from a friend.

Nothing.'

Gwen placed the sheet into a scanner and it transferred an image of a handprint to her monitor. Tiny lines blinked to the fingertips and palm, mapping the unique signatures and a series of images of other hand and fingerprints flashed up in a pop-up box as the Hub systems accessed similar records around the world.

Jack's impatience was palpable, and Gwen said after a minute, 'It takes time. Go have coffee. Ianto, make the man coffee.'

Ianto nodded and stood to go, but Jack waved him back to his seat. 'No coffee. No tea, no OJ, no vodka till we have answers.'

'I have a hit,' said Ianto shortly.

'Where?'

'Hang on…'

'Where!'

'Here. Sort of.' Ianto frowned. 'This doesn't make sense.'

'Let me judge that,' Jack said. 'Come on, what's up?'

Ianto looked back at the expectant Jack and Gwen. 'He's on the Torchwood database.'

'But that would mean…'

Ianto nodded at Gwen. 'Yeah, he's staff. But,' he added quickly, to stifle their questions, 'that's impossible. He's not on any records, no photos, no paper trail. Even Jack has a paper trail. The name doesn't show up anywhere, but that handprint is given top access here in Cardiff, at Canary Wharf, in Glasgow and at Torchwood Four. But no names, no pictures, no records whatsoever.'

Jack headed to his office. 'I'm going to talk to Archie in Glasgow. As a strange little old man himself, maybe he's an expert on even stranger little old men.' He slammed the office door behind him.

'You ever meet Archie?' Gwen asked Ianto.

Ianto shook his head.

'Owen?' she called down to the Autopsy Room.

'What now?'

'Ever met Archie?'

'Who?'

'Glasgow Archie,' Ianto added.

'Oh. Old Tartan Archie.' He appeared at the top of the stairs. 'Nah. Exchanged a few bizarre emails once.'

'Bizarre?'

'Yeah. Not sure he quite got the hang of computers really. Some of the words he used were... interesting and not always used in the right context. And he frequently referred to himself in the third person, so I thought he was a bit eccentric. Either that or the whisky was really good that morning.'

'I think we need a Torchwood day out to Glasgow. Take Archie out for a drink.'

'I'll hire a minibus,' Ianto said. 'Probably get it painted matt black quite easily.'

'Can we go without the blue lights this time. Sometimes, in the SUV, I feel like I'm in Santa's Grotto.' Owen headed back to work.

'I like the blue lights, me,' Gwen said. 'What's wrong with blue lights?'

Ianto shrugged. 'I think they look sophisticated. Perhaps Owen's only happy if they're red lights.'

Gwen laughed.

Jack came out of the office.

'Blue lights, Jack?' Gwen asked. 'Or red?'

Jack stared at the two of them. 'Sometimes, I'm not sure that office doesn't lead to a parallel dimension and each Hub I go into is slightly different from the one I left.'

'I think Jack's a blue light guy,' said Ianto. 'Look at the coat. And those matching shirts.'

'Oh, the shirts, yeah, dead giveaway,' Gwen agreed.

'Owen?' bellowed Jack. 'Have you been experimenting with strange gasses again?'

'Nope,' Owen yelled back. 'They're just weird, those two. I got used to it, why haven't you? Oh and Ianto, I prefer green lights, not red.'

Gwen gave Ianto an 'ooh, caught out' look and laughed.

Ianto winked at her, then called to Jack. 'Anything from Archie?'

'Nothing. Couldn't reach him. Maybe he needs a Ianto to field his calls.'

Ianto pretended to think about this. 'Cardiff or Glasgow? One's a nice city, with a nice Torchwood base near the waterside redevelopment, good shops and an enigmatic leading man who's never around when you want him. Or Cardiff? What should I do, Gwen?'

'Bet Archie doesn't have an SUV though.'

'Oh, good point. And I'm good on coffee, but I can't tell the difference between whisky and whiskey.'

'Oh, word puns,' said Jack at his left ear. 'Very good. Now, if you can apply some of that smartness to finding Tosh or Bilis, I'll take you out tonight and show you a good time.' Ianto turned to say something but Jack beat him to it. 'Yeah, I know, no rooftops.'

Ianto tried again. 'Photo?'

Jack raised an eyebrow.

'We could send a photo of Bilis to Glasgow,' said Ianto.

Jack snorted. 'Ever tried emailing an image to Archie? Either it bounces back, or he presses the wrong button and it ends up on the front page of the *Glasgow Herald*.'

'Oh, that's where that Loch Ness Monster story came from. I thought they were a bit close to the truth,' Ianto said.

'Loch Ness Monster? Do I want to know?' Gwen asked.

'Some kind of dinosaur, apparently,' said Owen, walking towards them with a PDA. 'Never believed that myself. Dinosaurs, God, whatever next?'

'We have a pterodactyl!' Gwen said, pointing upwards.

'Pteranodon, actually,' corrected Ianto. 'But Pterodactyl does sound sexier.'

Gwen sighed. 'Sometimes, I think I'm going mad.'

Jack clapped his hands. 'Tension-breaking banter over, guys. Serious jobs here. I want Bilis Manger. More importantly, I want Tosh safe and sound. And I kinda know you do, too, so let's say nothing more on the subject. Ianto, thank you for the research, I'm going to plough through more of it now. You and Gwen get out to Tretarri, see if she's there.' And then he looked hard at them and spoke softly. 'And yeah, I read that ghost-sighting report. And yeah, I think it's got something to do with this, so start your search at number 6, Coburg Street, OK? Owen, what've you got for me? I want to be able to pay a house call to Tretarri as soon as possible.'

'Do you believe in ghosts?' Ianto asked Gwen as they approached Tretarri in the SUV.

She shrugged. 'Well, we kind of know that most ghosts are time echoes rather than the "I'm haunting you, Ebenezer Scrooge" types, so no, I don't believe in ghosts per se.' She thought about that. 'Better to say, I don't believe in malicious hauntings.'

'Me neither. So why am I terrified of going into Tretarri?'

Gwen looked at him as he drove. 'My God, you are.'

Ianto was sweating profusely and was looking decidedly green around the gills. 'I don't know why,' he moaned. 'I know this is completely irrational, I keep saying to myself this is completely irrational but I'm pretty much bricking it.' He looked at her quickly. 'Sorry.'

She held a hand up. 'Not a problem. You want me to drive?'

'No, nearly there.' He pointed ahead. 'Years ago, there were plans to bulldoze this place, create a Cardiff Bay Retail Park rail station.'

'What happened?'

'Plans got bulldozed instead. How many Earth pennies d'you want to bet that if we found the sign-off form

124

blocking it, it'd have Bilis's signature on the bottom?'

'Oh I think you'd win that one fair and square.'

Ianto stopped the SUV near the retail park and suggested they walk the rest of the way. They went past the gasometer, and Gwen noticed the giant furniture store where Rhys had wanted to buy that hideous cream leather sofa. Apparently, he'd always liked the Swedes – although she was gratified to learn when they were at uni that he wasn't a great fan of Abba, since men at uni who were Abba fans tended not to be interested in Gwen. Or women generally. 'Do you like Abba?' she found herself asking Ianto. As non sequiturs went, it was a good one.

He looked at her. 'Is this going to lead to a "Jack" conversation?'

'No.'

'Fine. Then I admire the Andersson/Ulvaeus writing partnership as craftsmen and songsmiths. I believe "One Of Us" may be the best song written about relationship break-ups ever, and I have a soft spot for the fusion of witty lyrical content and poptastic danceability of "Voulez-Vous", but let me make this absolutely clear: I bloody loathe "Dancing Queen". All right?'

Gwen stopped walking and just looked at him.

'What?' he asked.

'You've had this conversation before, haven't you?'

'Might have.'

'Jack?'

'You honestly think Jack knows anything about music after 1948?'

'Who then?'

'Doesn't matter.'

'Who?' She starting walking again. 'Come on. I might die tonight, never knowing.'

'Me mam.'

'Aww. When she found out about Jack?'

'When I was fourteen.'

Gwen stopped again. 'I dunno which scares me more – that your mam worked you out ten years before you did, or that the fourteen-year-old Ianto Jones used the phrase "poptastic danceability" without getting beaten up.'

Ianto stopped suddenly. 'She didn't work me out, Gwen. No one has. And if I ever do, I'll let you know.'

Gwen smiled, nudged his arm. 'Oh come on, smile. Lisa, Jack... being bisexual is hardly a crime. Best of both worlds, isn't it?'

And Ianto pushed her away. 'No, Gwen. No, really it's bloody not. It's the worst of any world because you don't really belong anywhere, because you are never sure of yourself or those around you. You can't trust in anyone, their motives or their intentions. And because of that, you have, in a world that likes its nice shiny labels, no true identity. For Torchwood's "Little Miss Sensitive", you don't half talk crap sometimes. So do me a favour and shut up about it, all right?'

They didn't speak again till they reached Tretarri.

Gwen had planned to make straight for Coburg Street, but now she was wondering if it would be better to let Ianto take charge for once. She had been stung by his response, but she was also a bit alarmed. Ianto, the least highly strung of the team, seemed to be really ready to fly off the handle. She hoped that was something to do with the Tretarri effect and not a symptom of anything deeper.

'Where shall we start?' he said suddenly.

Gwen pointed down Coburg Street. 'You up for a bit of ghost-hunting?'

'No, but let's go anyway. I want to find Tosh.'

They made their way down the darkened streets, wary and alert. Ianto knelt down to the pavement. 'Freshly laid brickwork, and these uplighters are new, too.'

'Gonna look nice when it's all lit up, then,' said Gwen.

'Why here, though? I mean there are areas in Cardiff that need this treatment more than this old place. Places where real people live real lives.' Ianto straightened up, and tapped a notice taped to a lamp-post. 'Big street party, tomorrow at midday.' He stopped and looked about them. 'Gwen, this is weird.'

'Why?'

'I was here yesterday. With Jack. None of this was done, it was still a wreck. How do you renovate an entire block like this in one day?'

'With skill, expertise and a degree of savoir faire.'

They had their guns drawn and aimed at Bilis Manger before he'd finished speaking.

'Oh my,' he said. 'You do seem to always want to point guns at me. And I don't really see the need.'

'Where's Toshiko Sato?' demanded Gwen.

'Safe.'

'Yeah, cos I'm really gonna believe that.'

Bilis walked towards her and Gwen found that she couldn't take her eyes off him, couldn't fire her gun, couldn't move.

Her eyes flicked sideways. Ianto was the same, a statue, looking ahead, even though Bilis was parallel to him now, next to her.

'Let me show you how safe she is,' he purred and clicked his fingers.

Some way away, the door to number 6 opened, and Gwen could see a figure walking down the steps, almost as if in a trance.

It was Toshiko, though. Gwen knew that from her outline, the slight sashay to her steps. And she gasped as Toshiko turned towards them.

Half her face, her right, was painted white, and her eye had livid red streaks, outlined in gold, three going up, three down, like fire, or blood. And her lips were whitened, too. And there was something in the way she stood…

Gwen wanted to call out to her, but her mouth wouldn't work. And now she couldn't even blink.

'It's a trap you see,' Bilis whispered in her ear. 'A trap for the man you call Captain Jack Harkness, but known to me as… Well, no, that's between us. And you, Gwen Elisabeth Cooper, you are the bait.'

He reached over and eased the gun out of her hand and held it aloft. It vanished, just as she'd seen Bilis himself do before. Then Bilis stepped right into her field of vision, obscuring both Ianto and Tosh.

His eyes were gone, replaced by a blazing white light that seemed so strong it was going to burn its way out of his skull.

'The war between the Dark and the Light is never ending, Gwen. And I can only apologise – if there was any way I could avoid doing this, I would strive to find it. But I can't. I'm as much a victim in this as you.'

He took her hands in his. And leaned right in to her face, his white eyes roaring with the power contained there.

'I'm sorry. I am really very sorry.'

FOURTEEN

Ianto Jones was screaming inside. And there was nothing he could do; he couldn't move, couldn't seem to blink.

He was aware Bilis was close to Gwen, but couldn't turn to see what he was doing.

Then he saw Toshiko, half her face painted white. And red.

Bilis entered his field of vision.

'What have you done to Gwen?' Ianto shouted internally, but his mouth, his vocal cords, possibly even his lungs, weren't moving.

What had Bilis done? How had he done it?

Ianto's gun just vanished. One second it was there, the next he could feel it was gone.

Feel. So he could still feel, which meant that his nerves worked, which meant that muscles worked on some basic level which meant—

'Oh, do stop fretting,' Bilis smiled. 'So much noise in your head. And so many histories tell us that, in your brief

Torchwood career, they always thought you were the quiet one. The one who wouldn't say "boo" to a goose. I wonder if they ever knew you, Ianto. I wonder if Jack Harkness ever knew you.'

Ianto felt Bilis take his hands.

'I don't want to do this, you have to believe that. But there is a good reason. A very good reason. Good for me, anyway. You see, one man's light is another man's dark.' He squeezed Ianto's hands. 'But for what it's worth, I'm awfully sorry.'

As Bilis leaned in, Ianto got a glimpse of Toshiko. The white make-up seemed somehow alive, stretching right across her face. The last he saw of her, her whole face had become white: white skin, white lips; the only colour was the livid red and gold tearing from above and below her closed eyes. Her hair was moving, bunching, and, on either side of her head, hanging from the front of her hair, two cloth rollers. At the back were two long pins, forming the top of an X at the back of her head.

Then Bilis's head blotted out Ianto's view, and all he could see was the old man's face obscured by a fierce light that raged across his face, leaping from his eyes.

And Ianto was screaming again.

Jack stood inside the great Victorian morgue that dominated the basement area many levels beneath the Autopsy Room. He was facing that special row of trays that contained past Torchwood members.

According to Ianto's notes, Tray 18 was designated for

Gregory Phillip Bishop, who was reported dead in late 1941. Of course there was no body in the tray, but Ianto wouldn't have known that.

At least Jack hoped Ianto didn't know that. If he did, it would suggest a somewhat unhealthy obsession with frozen bodies, and that was an area even Jack didn't venture into.

'Gotta have some standards,' he thought wryly.

With a deep breath, Jack looked at Tray 78 (most of the Trays were deliberately non-sequential to prevent someone grave-robbing an entire Torchwood team's past in one fell swoop).

'Hello, Dr Brennan,' he said quietly to the tray marked up as Matilda B Brennan. 'It's been a while. I wish I could speak with you, find out why you made a deal with the devil. Wonder if you knew who or what Bilis Manger was back then. And if you did, I sure as hell wish you could tell me now.'

He wrenched the tray out, knowing what he'd find in the black body bag. After all, he'd helped Rhydian clear up after the event, so he'd actually placed Tilda's corpse in there.

The alien cryo-tech that Torchwood used to freeze the dead was something Jack had never truly understood. He doubted anyone had, least of all Charlie Gaskill's team that had first discovered and utilised it in 1906. Nevertheless, Jack knew it was an important part of their arsenal – one day, a way might be found to bring back an operative who could help a current case. It was something, like an early death, all Torchwood staff were prepared for.

Tilda Brennan wouldn't be brought back – being minus the top half of your head kind of ruled that out – but it wasn't her body he wanted. It was the scorched remains of the diary he'd secreted there with her, knowing that one day the 'Revenge for the Future' schtick would come back and haunt him.

And here it was. In the form of the enigmatic Bilis Manger, time-hopping killer and bon vivant, charm and danger all contained in the apparently frail body of an old man.

They'd first met in 1941, and again when Bilis had released Abaddon, but Jack still had no idea who the man actually was. He seemed human enough, so he got his abilities (Jack refused to think of them as powers, that sounded like something out of a comic book) from somewhere else. Bilis worshipped Abaddon, and Jack had destroyed 'the Great Devourer', but there had to be more to it than that. This was no two-bit villain with one ambition in life – he was simply too good for that.

A mercenary? A man from the future, living in the past? A really, really well-disguised alien?

The solution that nagged at Jack's conscious mind more than any other was the most disturbing. What if Bilis was a Torchwood officer, not from Cardiff (Ianto had checked, double-checked and checked forty times more) but from Glasgow? From the Institute in London? Or, God help them, from Torchwood Four. That wasn't a pretty thought.

He'd demonstrated the ability to plant false images of the future into people's heads. Poor Gwen had fallen for it when

Bilis told her Rhys was going to die – and then killed him, knowing that Gwen would open the Rift to bring him back (which it had – but bringing Abaddon along for the ride). He knew from conversations with the others that they'd seen the people that they most missed from their pasts come back too, solid projections that Bilis had controlled and manipulated, suggesting a deep-rooted knowledge of his team. And also the ability to spy on them as, in Owen's case, the image he'd seen had been of someone he'd lost so very recently.

So, he knew what Bilis could do, just not why and how.

'Great investigator, Jack,' he muttered. 'I thought "Revenge for the Future" referred to Abaddon. But what if it's more?'

He tapped his ear, activating the almost invisible communications device everyone in Torchwood wore. 'Owen?'

'Yeah?'

'Watcha doing?'

'Testing your blood for those chronon particles you asked about. Whatever they are. I mean, I know what they are, theoretically, but forgive me for being a doctor – and a bloody good one at that – but I like to work with realities rather than fantasy.'

'You wound me, Owen,' laughed Jack. 'What am I if not your fantasy?'

'A right pain in the arse, Jack, that's what you are. And I don't mean that in a way you'd find charming, before you ask. What do you want?'

'I'm heading out. I've read everything Ianto found for me and have a few ideas zooming about my head, but I need more. I need to find me an expert on old books. And I know just the guy.'

'See yas,' said Owen and broke comms.

Jack took one of the back routes out of the base, bypassing the Hub and walking up a long, long (really quite long) flight of stairs that brought him out behind Ianto's tourist information office. He went through the little room and out into the night air.

People were milling around by the big pub above the doorway, whilst others were flocking to the Turkish restaurant that stood over the water. There was the faux French restaurant (good chain, Jack quite liked the flans and quiches they did), a couple of Italians on the upper level, and a number of bars, coffee houses and, down Bute Street, a series of shops, galleries and even a comedy club.

Fifty years ago, he'd walked an alien disguised as an evacuee child along here, all mud flats and dampness. The warehouse that the Hub was accessed by in 1941 had long since been demolished, and roughly where it stood there was now a pizza parlour. Whenever Jack went in there, it always seemed to be full of very tall Welshmen with booming voices, entertaining their diminutive Welsh mothers, with their soft sing-song voices. Jack loved Wales, the Welsh, the whole spirit and pizzazz of the place. If he had to spend 150 years somewhere on Earth, there were worse places he could've gone.

Imagine if there'd been a space-time rift in Swindon.

Of course Swindon was quite nice, and certainly had an interesting roundabout system that could fool any passing aliens, but Torchwood Swindon didn't have the right ring to it.

Or the nice bay.

Jack passed the bars and hotels of Bute Street, stopped off at Jubilee Pizza (not as nice as the restaurant in the Bay, obviously, but faster for takeaway) and towards one of the recent housing developments, Century Wharf, a strange riverside collection of apartments that could never quite make up its mind if it was in Butetown or Grangetown – not that it really mattered greatly.

He wandered into the gated community, his wrist-strap controls overriding the electronic 'Residents Only' security system, and headed towards the block he wanted.

He buzzed the number, knowing that it had a video entryphone and he'd get short shrift once the occupant saw who he was.

Charm offensive, Jack. Gets 'em every time.

'Hey, it's me,' he said when the buzzer was answered.

There was a beat, followed by a command to go away that could've been termed more politely.

'I brought dinner,' Jack added, and waved the pizza at the camera. 'Hawaiian, with extra mushroom.'

The door clicked and Jack was in. He took the stairs, and was soon on the fourth floor.

The door to the apartment was open, and Jack went in, noting the smell of freshly showered human male. A couple of uplighter lamps illuminated a large living room with three glass doors overlooking the River Taff and the city beyond, lit up like it was Christmas.

Idris was in a dressing gown, hair damp. He wasn't smiling.

'What do you want?'

Jack offered the pizza box, which Idris took and opened, yanking off a sliver and eating it.

'Yeah. Good food,' Idris said. 'So, what do you want?'

'A slice of pizza?'

'Get your own.' Idris ate another bit.

Jack pulled the book out of his coat pocket.

'I have people in trouble. I need answers about this book.'

'It's a diary,' Idris said without touching it. 'Broken lock, so personal. I imagine it's not yours.'

'It is now.'

Idris rinsed his hands in the sink, dried them thoroughly and sat down at the kitchen table, switching the overhead lights on.

He flicked quickly through the burnt diary, not bothering to comment on the damage.

'Well?'

Idris shrugged. 'Well what? You want first impressions? I'd have thought you had the technology at Torchwood to tell you everything you needed to know.'

'Those people in trouble? One of them's Toshiko Sato. She'd be the one to tell me what I'm having to ask you.'

Idris frowned. 'Japanese girl, parents used to be something in the military. She used to be at some low-rated

MoD place, yeah?'

'You know my staff?'

'I know my job,' Idris snapped. 'Keeping a step ahead of you is impossible, but knowing who your people are, that's a work in progress.' He tapped the diary. 'Overlooking its charred state, it's a diary. Probably Edwardian, the cover's faux leather, the locking mechanism, a bit later, 1920s perhaps, replacing the original.'

'The paper?'

'That's why you need an expert. It feels normal enough, but I doubt you'd have brought it to me if it was.'

Jack shrugged. 'I honestly don't know. And I thought you might be enough of an expert to tell me.'

Idris shut the book. 'I collect books, Jack. Sometimes I sell them on eBay, or buy others. I'm not a bloody humanoid Google. Yeah, it's paper, it's thick enough to be early 1900s, and it's not treated like modern paper, hence the discolouration and brittleness. The edges are gilt – not real gilt, so it's probably not the most expensive diary. The sort a maiden aunt might have given to a young boy or girl in an upper-middle-class family. You want a value? In good nick, £100 thereabouts. Damaged like this, it's recycling only.'

Jack shrugged. 'Shame it got burned. With all those blank pages, you could write in it. Keep a diary of all your conquests, Idris. Then I could read it.'

Idris sighed at the implicit entendre. He threw the book back to Jack, and fished out another slice of pizza, so Jack knew he wasn't planning to touch the diary again.

'It's not blank,' the Welshman said after a few seconds' munching. 'Why'd you think that? I'm surprised at you.'

Jack flicked the crumbling pages. 'Looks empty to me.'

Idris finally cracked a smile. 'You might be good at aliens and stuff, Jack, but you're a shite boy scout.'

He went back to the kitchen and got a plastic lemon juice dispenser from the fridge. He squirted some onto kitchen roll and gently tapped a page in the diary.

Faintly, some scrawled words appeared. 'Old trick, old book. Lemon juice isn't great, but it should do the trick. But I suggest you copy down what it says quickly cos, as it dries, the words will go again, and it'll make the pages even more brittle. One good gust of wind, and they'll shatter.'

Jack smiled at him and put the diary down again. Next to it he placed the USB memory stick he'd been given in the park.

'How long?'

Idris snorted and repeated his earlier suggestion that Jack should go away, but Jack was insistent. 'Idris, Tosh's life is in danger. I've heard nothing from Ianto or Gwen. You're my only hope.'

Idris looked Jack straight in the eyes, and then sighed. 'If this was a movie, Harkness, I'd be sixty, bald and looking over my shoulder in case the Nazis burst in.'

'You'll never go bald.'

'Donald Pleasance. Or Laurence Naismith.'

Jack headed out the door. 'How long?'

'Three hours for a rough estimate.'

Jack looked back and smiled. 'Even those guys were

beautiful when they were your age. Probably. And Idris?'

'What?'

'Thank you.'

Jack pulled the door shut and headed back out into the night air. He crossed down towards the river, deciding to take the scenic route back to the Hub. It was a busy night and, for the sake of ten more minutes, strolling through Hamadryad Park would clear his mind, let him focus.

FIFTEEN

Owen Harper was on the verge of throwing the blood samples against the walls of the Autopsy Room. Somehow, flecking the white brickwork with red splatter seemed more worthwhile than what he was doing right now.

'I can't do it, Jack,' he yelled, knowing no one could hear him, cos the Hub was empty. 'Whatever you've got in your body, I can't isolate it!'

He kicked the autopsy table instead.

It was just as melodramatic, but less destructive. Although his left toes might not agree for the next minute or so.

'Stupid, stupid…'

He turned back to the screen projected on the white wall behind him. Jack's blood. Jack's DNA. Jack's tissue samples. If he'd had any, frankly, he'd have happily tested Jack's faeces, sperm, anything that might help find out what made Jack Harkness unique amongst mankind.

'Are you trying to find out what stops him going into

Tretarri?' asked a silky voice from above him. 'Or to isolate what actually makes him come back to life?'

Owen didn't look up into the Hub. He knew it was Bilis. The idea that the little old man could come and go no longer alarmed Owen. He took a deep breath and carried on working. 'If you've anything useful to add, tell me. Otherwise, piss off out of the Hub, I'm busy.'

And Bilis was in front of him, hands behind his back, smiling, head slightly cocked as if listening to something.

'There's a cry in your head, Owen,' he said. 'A sound. A connection. To our chum in the cells, and all the others out there.'

'Dunno what you're talking about, mate.'

'Yes you do,' Bilis said simply. 'You've known for a long time. But you don't tell anyone else, do you? Because it frightens you. You know there's something of the Weevil about you. On one level, it's just a post-traumatic thing. You identify with their bestiality, because you know that beneath the snarls, beneath the aggression, are intelligent, communal beings who need one another. And, like the Weevils, Owen Harper wants to believe he can survive alone, when what he really needs is a good hug.'

Owen just stared at Bilis, then forced a smile on his face. 'You should go into counselling, mate,' he said.

And he turned back to his blood samples, so Bilis wouldn't see the frown. A frown because Bilis, damn him, had a point.

Not so much the loneliness – Owen had got accustomed to that, but no, the Weevils thing. He did find he had some weird connection to them. And that scared him because he couldn't work out why he was drawn to them.

He felt Bilis's hand on his shoulder. 'I'm sorry Owen. It will make sense in the future. And for that, I am truly sorry.'

Owen shook the hand off. 'You are ten seconds away from being shot,' he said.

Bilis laughed a soft humourless laugh. 'Oh we know that's not going to happen. But other things are that will be life-changing for you. And I can't help you. No one can. Remember how fragile life is, Owen Harper. As a doctor, you know that. Learn to cherish it.'

And Owen saw something on the floor. A revolver, just lying there, a curl of smoke petering out above the barrel.

Then it was gone. And so was Bilis.

Owen searched the Hub, the lower levels, the upper levels and even the Boardroom, but no sign.

Exactly how he wound up in the Vaults, staring at the Weevil in its cell, he couldn't remember.

But now he was there, unaware that, as Bilis had earlier, he had pressed his hand against the plastic door. On the other side, the imprisoned Weevil pressed its own hand to the door.

'Why are you here?' Owen asked it. 'How do you cope in this alien environment?'

The Weevil said nothing.

Owen pulled back. Jesus, he was talking to Weevils. What was going on with him these days?

'Poor bloody thing,' he thought. 'Shoved into an alien

145

environment, a cage with so many security doors to stop you getting out to where you think you belong. Waiting for something to go wrong, waiting for the security systems to go down like before. Giving you access to the forbidden Hub and beyond that the wastelands of Cardiff, the sewers, the landfills, the—'

Of course! That was it, they'd been looking at this all the wrong way round.

Owen belted from the Vaults back to the Boardroom.

And that was his mistake – he was so determined to contact Jack, to warn him, because he'd figured it out.

Because he was Owen. Because he was always the fool who rushed in.

And because he never saw the bigger picture.

Never saw what was behind him.

'Jack,' he slammed his fist on the comms system, knowing that, wherever Jack had gone, he'd have his cochlear Bluetooth activated. 'Jack, listen to me!'

Nothing.

'Damn it, Jack, I hope you're just being bloody-minded and can hear me anyway. Listen, it's not that you can't get in, you can. There's nothing in you stopping you, it's deliberate. Not your body or anything. Tretarri itself is locked to you. You need a key… No, that's not it. It's… it's like a lockdown here – at some point, you are going to be let in, but on the town's terms! Shit, Jack, it's a trap waiting to be sprung. It's a trap and that's why it's got Tosh. She's bait, Jack. You've got to get back here – now!'

Nothing.

'Jack! For God's sake!'

'I knew it would be you,' said Bilis, standing behind him. 'You're so methodical, leaving nothing to chance. If at first he doesn't succeed, Owen Harper tries and tries again.'

Owen was round, ready to fight, but Bilis was so much faster.

'I blocked the comms system, sorry,' said Bilis, as he grabbed Owen's hands. 'If Jack tries to call in, he'll get Craig Armstrong's *Bolero*. I thought it suited his… taste for the debauched.'

Owen was expecting an easy fight – Bilis was what, seventy-five, eighty? Weedy, stick-like, bit theatrical?

But Owen was wrong, and Owen was on his knees, then prone in seconds as Bilis crushed his hands as if he were a pneumatic vice.

Owen heard a shriek of unendurable agony and realised it was his own voice, and then the darkness took him.

Jack liked the waterside. He walked along, watching the lights of the modern apartments opposite contrasting with the Victorian terraces behind him.

A couple of late-night ducks splashed in the water, and Jack leaned over to look at them. By now, the moon was up, a three-quarter orb in the sky, bright white, and it reflected on the largely unbroken waters, only the odd ducked-formed ripple fragmenting the image.

Jack thought of space. Of being up there. Out amongst the stars. He could have gone back, not long ago. He'd had the chance, but opted not to take it. Cardiff, specifically the team at Torchwood, needed him. Earth needed him. Every single one of these bizarre little people needed him. And damn it, he needed them, too. They made him feel alive, gave him a purpose, gave him a reason to live.

'Jack.'

He felt the word whispered in his ear, so softly it could almost have been the breeze. Except there wasn't one.

He shivered anyway.

And realised that there was someone beside him. He could see the reflection in the water.

'No,' said the voice. 'Don't turn around. Just listen. I'm trying, trying so hard to do everything you taught me, but it's difficult to maintain myself. It's got all four of them, Jack. There's just you now.'

The figure loomed forward and Jack saw a face. A young man, tall, dark-haired, blue-eyed (oh God, those beautiful eyes he hadn't seen for so long), the cheekbones he wanted to rest a coffee mug on. No toothy smile though. Just a pained expression.

Jack's heart literally jumped, and he breathed in sharply and deeply. 'Greg,' he breathed out.

'I'm sorry, Jack, it's so powerful. I'm really trying though… Please believe me.'

Jack stared at the reflection. He'd seen enough movies to know that, if he turned round, Greg would not be there.

'Is it Bilis Manger?'

Greg frowned. 'It's so bright. And so dark. And I don't know where I am, Jack. But it's got them. It's hurting them, Jack.'

'Is it Bilis Manger?' Jack spat, spinning round.

But Greg had gone.

Now it really had got cold. Damn the river, damn the park, damn the bloody ducks. He'd got distracted.

He ran, as fast as he could, across the park, up the steps onto the link road, across the roundabout and into Mermaid Quay.

By the time he reached Ianto's shop front, he knew he was too late.

Standing further back, by the ice-cream parlour over the water, was Bilis.

The shop had a huge iron bar across the doorway, held in place by a massive, almost comically huge, iron padlock.

Instinctively, Jack tapped his ear. 'Owen?' he barked.

Nothing. No, not nothing – music. That was a new one.

He looked over at Bilis. 'What have you done to Owen? Let me into the Hub!'

But Bilis was holding the padlock key in the air. He smiled, turned and threw it into the middle of the inner harbour. It vanished with a damp plop, and Bilis vanished as instantly.

Jack tried wrenching the bar off the door, but he knew it was futile.

He dashed up through Roald Dahl Plass to the water tower, activating the perception-filtered step/elevator via his wrist-strap as he ran, but when he got there, nothing happened.

People were staring at him as he jumped onto the step, ignoring water splashing around.

Damn, how could they see him?

Why wasn't he moving down?

Four or five bemused people were watching him now. Among them, he realised, was Bilis Manger. Bilis waved, turned his back and walked into the foyer of the Millennium Centre.

Jack hurled himself past the crowds and into the venue.

Everywhere there were people – it was fifteen minutes to curtain up, and there were crowds moving up the steps on the left to the massive auditorium of the Donald Gordon Theatre, and more people were sweeping through from the bars and cafés from the right, heading past the desks and to the same steps.

Jack tried to focus, but he knew that Bilis would already have gone.

'Mr Harkness?'

It was a maroon-waistcoated staffer, a collection of programmes for the show in his hand.

'Yeah?'

'The gentleman said you'd be here. He asked me to make sure you got your ticket. He's already gone in.'

Jack took the ticket, but didn't read it, instead looking towards the throng moving up the steps.

He was never going to able to confront Bilis in a theatre full of people.

'No, sir,' said the staffer, noting the direction Jack was gazing. 'The gallery exhibitions are up the right steps, Level 2, sir.' He pointed through the crowd in the direction of the bars.

Jack thanked him and eased himself slowly through the crowd, getting one or two hissed complaints as he stepped on a toe or knocked a handbag out of a manicured hand.

Eventually, he reached the wooden steps leading to the smaller galleries and conference rooms and took them three at a time.

He glanced at the ticket and read:

RECEPTION FOR THE TIME AGENCY.
UPPER BAR. GLANFA.

He threw himself into the bar, hand on his holster, expecting trouble.

Instead, he found a quiet, brightly lit bar, one barman and Bilis Manager, looking as cool and dapper as ever, sipping sherry from a glass, a waiter stood beside him, holding a tray of sherry glasses.

'Jack,' Bilis said expansively, as if welcoming an old friend to a party. 'Delighted you could make it.'

Jack still kept his hand on his gun, but slowed to a casual walk as he headed to where Bilis stood.

The old man toasted him and then nodded to the windows, which showed the reverse of the words cut into the front of the building. Jack looked out towards the water tower below.

'"In these stones, horizons sing." They are inspiring words, don't you think, Jack?'

Jack shrugged. 'What do you want?'

'Creating truth like glass from the furnace of inspiration

– written by Wales's first-ever national poet. Truth is a strange thing – one man's truth is another man's pack of lies.'

Jack turned away from Bilis. 'If you've nothing relevant to say, Bilis, I have a team to find.'

'Oh, you won't be able to do that, I'm afraid. They won't let you. Not yet. Tomorrow maybe, at the launch party.'

Jack turned back, walked to Bilis, ignoring the waiter, who staggered back as Jack cannoned into him. He grabbed Bilis by his red cravat, swallowing his surprise that the old man didn't just vanish.

But then, maybe he hadn't been expecting Jack to do that – so he could be surprised, caught unawares. Good.

'Talking of furnaces of inspiration, I'm damn well inspired to chuck you through the glass and see if you can vanish in mid-air. But you know, I don't think that would achieve anything. Where are they?'

'I honestly can't answer that, I'm awfully sorry.' Bilis freed himself and straightened his clothing. 'But I'm sure they are safe. I don't think they want to hurt them.'

'They?'

'The Light, Jack. The Light and the Dark – forever at war, battling across the dimensions for centuries, coming here through your blessed Rift. My Lord understood them, but you destroyed him. And when you did that, they were free to do as they wanted. Capricious elements, you might say.'

'What's your role in this?'

'I'm bound to them as I was bound to my Lord. I am but a humble servant – I see time, all time, past, present and so many potential futures. I can give you a glimpse of any number of futures, if you like, Jack. It'd keep you safely away. And give you so many clues.'

'To what?'

'To everything.'

Jack looked around the room. The waiter and barman were chatting at the bar, oblivious to the scene by the windows.

'What are you, Bilis?'

Bilis opened his mouth as if to answer, then stopped.

For the first time, Jack sensed... panic? Weakness?

'Losing the war, Jack,' Bilis said. 'Maybe not the battle, but the war. This is the century, Jack, remember?'

He put his hand into his pocket and produced a locket on a chain.

Jack frowned – he was sure he'd seen that before. Where?

Bilis pocketed it again. 'Anyway, Captain Jack Harkness, I do hope you can join me tomorrow at the grand opening of Tretarri. It's been a party in the making for so long.'

Jack shook his head. 'Seems to me you turned everything around real quick.'

Bilis grinned. 'Oh my dear Captain, how little you understand. But you will. You will.'

And Bilis was gone.

So were the staff. Jack stood in the semi-darkness. The bar was shuttered, and there was no sign anyone had been in the room for hours.

My story starts with the earthquake of 1876, four years past. It was only a minor inconvenience to most, few realised what it was or that it seemed centred on my beloved Tretarri.

But I knew. I knew the truth, for there were no natural fires that night. No, instead, the great gods of the underworld tore their way through to the surface of our small planet, their eternal fights and battles spilling over into our reality.

And only I was there to pay witness to these events, to commune with the demons therein and their pitiful servants.

But I get ahead of myself. It was a normal eve, as I recall — as normal as any had been since my beloved Marjorie had been taken from me. The families of Tretarri were at St Paul's Church, in Grangetown, but

I had foresworn Our Lord and his ministries since losing Marjorie.

I stood at the heart of the village as the ground began to shake, and smoke belched from the ground.

I believed my time had come, that I would not survive the next few moments, and I began to think of Marjorie. I find it interesting that, even in those seconds of terror, not once did I offer prayer or give thought to the Lord God above.

And the streets were split asunder by a huge fire and crimson smoke, while bizarre phantasmagorias of lights and other energies could be seen amidst the smoke.

The sounds were deafening but, as I later learned, no one outside the village heard or saw anything, although the fires that night drew the attention of the constabulary and other authorities who believed it to be a straightforward fire in number 6 Coburg Street. And, in fear of my sanity and my standing, I am ashamed to say I never gave them cause to think otherwise.

I am just eternally grateful that no innocent souls were lost that night.

'Souls'. How easily I write such words, and yet believe in them not.

I hid in the doorway of a home on Bute Terrace, lost in mute fear of that which I was seeing, as a massive hand, the size of a horse and carriage, erupted from within the vast crack that had split the road asunder. Grey, taloned – I remember every detail right down to the ridges on the knuckles, so terrified was I that it is burned upon my memory for, I fear, the rest of my days. The fearsome claws raked across the road, getting a grip to enable the rest of its foul body to haul itself upwards, the reddish smoke still crackling and dancing around above, rivulets of lights darting across its path, as if each sparkle were a life of its own.

An arm, a shoulder and then a mastiff-like head reared up, ignoring me but belching fire, snarling and retching its foulness into our air.

At the far end of the street, a second identical creature appeared, this one a royal blue in colour, in the same stage of emergence.

And that was when I observed two men, both in their later years, just standing at either end of Bute Terrace, as if standing Second for the two inhuman duellists.

I am taken with the fancy that they not only stood and dressed with the bearing of men alike but, facially, they may have been twins. I confess my attention was not on them for very long, but my instinct is to say they were identical twins. I cannot offer any evidence to back this up other than my memories of brief observation.

The Seconders for these Beasts raised their hands in unison, and the crimson energy about our heads became a whirlpool of incredible power, I could feel the air being drawn from my body and feared I would die there in the street, but the Beasts, only their heads and shoulders above ground, now turned to face one another, sending rocks and earth into the air as they did so.

The tiny lights within the crimson storm darted about, some with the Grey Beast, some garnered with the Blue Beast, and I understood that what I witnessed was beyond the ken of mortal man. Truly, I was seeing a battle of the darkest order.

Energies flew about the Beasts' heads, although they moved little, other than to twist their heads and roar inhuman words at one another. The main warring seemed to be between the lights in the storm, the ones nearest the Blue Beast had now become solid blackness rather than the brightness of the Grey Beast's allies. Light versus Dark.

'Indeed,' said a voice beside me.

I realised the Seconder for the Grey Beast was beside me. He explained he was known as Bilis Manger; he believed he embodied the Pain of the Devourer, whatever that meant. He referred to his opposite as Cafard Manger, perhaps confirming my view they were related, or twins even. I never had the opportunity to enquire, for this Bilis entrusted me with a task.

He explained that the fair City of Cardiff was home

to these Beasts, and had been since the dawn of creation. Something called a Rift splintered through the land, I gathered this to be the crimson smoke about our heads, and that the two Beasts were fighting for control of it.

Or to escape it.

He passed me this book and a special pen of a kind I had never seen before. He said it would write words but I would not be able to read them back.

He said it was essential that I wrote today's events down in this diary – and nothing else.

And that when the day was won or lost by one of the Beasts and its Seconder, I was to seal this diary up and ensure it was buried here in Cardiff with me.

I pointed out that it was likely I would be leaving Cardiff soon, that, without Marjorie, I had no reason to stay in my adopted hometown, but Bilis was insistent. It mattered not where I travelled, provided that I was buried here in Cardiff. In St Mary's churchyard, which was in a remote part of north Cardiff.

But I should tell you of the battle – except that I am, to be honest, ignorant of what exactly occurred. A lot of growling by the Beasts and a lot of back and forth by the black and white lights.

Bilis Manger and the other Seconder did nothing until, after about five minutes, the crimson storm flared very brightly, the white lights winked away and the Blue

Beast rose up higher and the Grey one vanished beneath the ground.

With a final roar, the Blue Beast beat his chest like some giant ape from the dark continents, and it too vanished through the gaping crack from whence it came and the hole sealed up, and the crimson storm was gone.

The two Seconders remained – the one I know to be Cafard walked towards Bilis. They shook hands, and, in the strangest piece of hokum ever, Cafard seemed to press against Bilis and vanish, almost as if, somehow, he were inside the man I had spoken to.

Bilis said one last thing to me.

He said Tretarri was no longer mine, nor was it for the workers. He said they should all be out of their homes within seven days, or he would not be responsible for the consequences. But I did not take this as a threat, more of an apology. I got the impression this rather dear man was concerned for their wellbeing.

Having witnessed the battle of the Beasts, I could only agree.

I asked Bilis what he would do now – the Beast he worked for was seemingly defeated.

He told me, and I remember his words so clearly: 'I walk through the eternity of past, present and possible futures, until such time as my Lord Abaddon is reborn. Until then, you, Gideon ap Tarri, must remember two things. Firstly, the word "Torchwood", for it will destroy the future. And secondly, that I, Bilis Manger, shall seek the ultimate revenge for the future. Because it must not come to pass – and yet without my Lord Abaddon, it will.'

I never saw him again.

Over the next week, I re-housed my loyal workers in newer accommodations in the Windsor and Bute Esplanades.

Only once more did I try to visit Tretarri but something there kept me out. Not physically, but I was afeared when I entered it, my heart palpitated, and my throat was parched in a second. I could not rationalise this, but I know and respect fear and swore never to return.

As bidden by Bilis Manger, who disappeared from my life that day and has never returned, I have written this down four years hence.

I have made it a stipulation of my Last Will and Testament that this diary shall be buried with me. I am placing it within a wooden box in my attic. Today will be the last time I ever see it.

Gideon ap Tarri
12 June 1880

I have recourse to retrieve this diary and, for the sake of Bilis Manger if ever he finds it, make note of the events of this afternoon.

A man approached me, a Scots man I believe. He claimed he represented Her Majesty Queen Victoria. He gave me no name, but he had a military bearing along with the uniform, so I had no reason no doubt his claim.

He asked, nay, demanded the diary.

When I feigned ignorance, he explained he was from the Torchwood Institute in London.

Bilis, my friend, I cannot say for sure if this diary will now be buried with me, for I feel I must flee, if only to draw this Torchwood away from the diary. If we remain in one another's company, they shall I am sure locate it.

I hope, desperately hope, that my panic is for nought and I shall return to Cardiff shortly.

But today, I am headed away from here. I shall not say where.

This may be my last entry.

God be with you

Gideon Tarry, formerly Gideon Haworth Esq
18 September 1881

SIXTEEN

Rhys Williams glanced at the clock on the wall: 11.46am. He adjusted his tie in the mirror, and brushed a bit of dust off the collar of his Savile Row suit. Neatness mattered.

Alone in the room, he slipped the jacket off and took a side-on look at himself. 'Thirty-two-inch waist for the first time since you were eighteen, Rhys Alun Williams,' he said proudly. 'Not bad for a man getting closer to the wrong side of thirty-five.'

'Too true, Mister Sexy Pants,' Gwen said, emerging from the en suite.

Rhys took her, all of her, in his arms, and they kissed. Passionately. Longingly. Slowly, he led her towards the bed.

She broke off, laughing. 'Calm down, lover,' she said, patting her extended belly. 'Not till junior is out and running about.'

'Running about?' Rhys put on a mock stressed expression. 'He won't be playing for the Torchwood IX Under-10s for another few years. I have to wait till then?'

They laughed. 'About another three hours,' Gwen said, 'and I'm all yours again.'

Rhys was serious. 'Gwen, God knows I've hated Torchwood and I've loved Torchwood, but right now I'm scared of Torchwood.'

'Oh, not again…'

'I'm serious. OK, so this alien technology you lot found, yeah, it guarantees safe delivery, yeah, it negates caesareans and breeches or whatever, but…'

'But it's still alien tech, and you don't like it.'

Rhys looked down at his feet. 'Jack didn't like it,' he said quietly.

Gwen just stood there, all passion and love drained in a second. She sat in the chair at the dresser, refusing to look directly at Rhys, instead directing her voice at his reflection. 'Jack isn't here any more.'

Rhys wouldn't catch her eye. 'He didn't trust the dependency on alien tech, Gwen, and, for all his faults, I trusted Jack's integrity, if not his morality. If something goes wrong—'

'Nothing will go wrong, Rhys, for crying out loud. Owen tested it! Owen, the man you were happy enough to let save my life once before.'

'I saved you!'

'Using his alien tech! If it was good enough then—'

Rhys leapt up. 'That was an emergency, Gwen. That was life and death. That was the most terrifying day of my bloody life, and I had no choice but to trust Owen Bloody Harper. Now, now I have a choice!'

Gwen spun round on him. 'No! No, Rhys, you don't. I'm doing this because I'm the one facing hours of labour, I'm the one facing depression and illness and pain. I'm the one facing the possibility that, after nine months carrying this baby, something could go wrong and it dies. Or I die.'

'Our baby,' Rhys muttered, not caring whether Gwen heard him or not.

'So, yeah, I'm happy to use technology that guarantees one hundred per cent a healthy boy and a healthy mum. I'd have thought my darling husband would be happy at that thought.'

Rhys knew he'd lost. 'I do, love, believe me. I just think that what my mam said about natural birth—'

And Gwen was up and heading out of the bedroom.

'Brenda Bloody Williams and her pre-natal care. If there's anything that almost stopped me getting pregnant, it was knowing that at the back of every decision we made your mother would be saying, "Oh, I'm not sure that's the way to hold a baby," or "Are you really dressing him in that," or "Are you sure that's the right food for a baby," or "In my day, children were seen and not heard." Screw you, Rhys and screw your mam too!'

With a loud slam of the door, she was out, clattering down the stairs.

No, not stopping at the next level, going all the way down to the front door.

SLAM.

Gone.

Rhys sighed to himself, checked his tie again, slipped the jacket on and followed her downstairs, through the front door and out to the car.

She was sitting in the passenger seat. He slid into the driving seat.

'Alien tech, eh?' he said. 'Can save all those pains, can't do a bloody thing about your hormones, can it?'

Gwen stared at him. 'Shut up.'

'I mean, cos that'd be really useful wouldn't it. "Hi, I'm Owen Harper, I can give something really useful to the world. Hormonal balance." Now that would be an improvement.'

'Shut up.'

'I mean, look at the time. In thirty minutes, we'll have a baby boy, happy, healthy and perfect in an Orwell-would-have-hated-it way. But after all that, I bet you'll still be grumpy, unpredictable, eating raw pickles by the cartload and phoning me at the office and accusing me of shagging Ruth.'

'Shut up.' A beat. 'Which one's Ruth?'

Rhys used his hands to suggest a somewhat large lady.

'Oh, that Ruth, from Harwoods? Ruth, now your staff liaison officer?'

'That's the one.'

'Well, if I thought you were humping Ruth, my hormones would be the least of your problems. Now, can you get me to St Helen's maternity wing in the next thirty minutes or shall I have the natural birth you so desperately want all over the insides of your Porsche?'

Rhys pressed the ignition switch. The car roared into life, and he eased it away from the front door and down the long drive.

He flicked a button on the dash, and the security gates started to open. Two armed Torchwood guards in the gatehouse waved politely as he steered out into the midday sun and on their journey towards Cardiff and the birth of their baby.

'I sometimes think,' Rhys said, checking no one was following them, 'that those guards Tosh gave you are as much to keep us in as to guard us.'

'You worry too much.'

'I worry that if the Torchwood Empire is so beneficial to mankind, then why do we need protecting and who from?'

'From whom,' Gwen corrected.

'Ooh, get the girl from Swansea and her posh English.' Rhys adjusted the rear-view mirror as they trundled through the outer areas of the city.

'Not sure I like this area, Rhys,' Gwen said. 'Isn't there a better route? Through Whitchurch?'

Rhys gritted his teeth, knowing that he was going to get shouted at again.

'Dunno, Gwen. I think it does us all good to take the odd trip through the less fortunate ends of the Empire, see how the other half live. I mean, I know mothers aren't your preferred choice of subject, but if yours was still here I'm not sure she'd approve of what we've become.'

Gwen put a hand on Rhys's. 'It's not like that, love. I didn't plan this. You didn't plan to run the Council, we never planned for Torchwood to create an empire, but history tells us that to create a Utopia, a bit of darkness has to be present, to make the light glow stronger.'

Rhys said nothing and they drove in silence, until the sat-nav spoke, telling them they were thirteen minutes away from St Helen's Hospital.

'When Tosh and Owen finish the project, Rhys, I promise you, the world that baby Gareth inherits will be one that has made all this worthwhile.'

Rhys put his foot down and, before long, they were approaching the hospital, a group of Torchwood guards and nursing staff greeting them.

As they pulled up, Rhys looked at his wife, and then nodded to the group outside. 'When I married you, I imagined an NHS hospital, me pacing the corridors for eight hours drinking weak-as-piss tea, and Jack stood there, winding me up saying it was an alien. Or his. Or both. But I love you so much, and I trust that you know what you're doing. Even without Jack Bloody Harkness to guide us all.'

Gwen kissed him on the cheek. 'I'll text you when he's been born.'

'One last thing, love,' Rhys said as the car door opened. 'I never agreed to Gareth. I reckon Geraint. After your dad. Good name, good thing for our boy to live up to.'

And Gwen grabbed him and kissed him savagely and powerfully.

Rhys eased her away, embarrassed. The assembled staff outside were applauding them in that way that Torchwood staff always applauded.

Nauseatingly, and slightly insincerely.

Jack Harkness would have hated this new Torchwood.

And then Gwen was out of sight, inside the building.

Rhys eased the car out of the car park then drove towards the city. He needed to get to work for a late-night session about what to do with the irradiated Bay. Ever since the Hub had exploded, the whole area had been in desperate need of reclamation.

As he drove, Rhys pulled a Bluetooth earpiece from his pocket, slipped it on and spoke to the sat-nav.

'Override Torchwood comms. Clearance five stroke nine.'

'Confirmed. Signal scrambled.'

'Connect me with Friend 16.'

'Confirmed.'

There was a buzz and then a click.

A Welsh voice spoke, curtly, passionless. 'What do you want, Williams?'

'Gwen is safe. If you're going to do it, please do it now.'

The line went dead.

SEVENTEEN

Jack was at a loss – not a feeling he was particularly familiar with. With no way to access the Hub, unless he could get an acetylene torch at nearly midnight, and with no team to support him, he really didn't have a clue what to do next. Or where to go.

Ianto's? Nope, key in the drawer in his office. Gwen's? Yeah, Rhys would love that – he'd probably been phoning and texting Gwen all evening and be worried enough as it was that he'd had no response.

Both Toshiko and Owen had moved recently to new apartments, and neither of them had offered him a key, so that was out.

Idris? Nope, he'd probably worn out what passed for a welcome there.

He was standing by the water tower, looking across at the parade of restaurants and bars in Mermaid Quay and Bute Street. He wasn't much of a drinker, but perhaps there was a late-night bar.

The Sidings, of course. Bit of a trek, but there'd be a welcome there. Of sorts. Mind you, the last time he'd gone there, he'd been stalked by a Hoix. It had got through the Sidings' defences and… Well, perhaps the welcome wouldn't be that welcoming after all.

Bottom line was, Jack was furious with himself. He'd been hoodwinked by someone – someone really quite disarming and elegant, yet powerful. His team had been trapped (he was assuming Owen wasn't locked inside the Hub; somehow that didn't seem Bilis's style), and he had no idea why or how to find and free them.

Suddenly, Jack was angry. And that usually meant that the last thing he needed right now was people, bars, noise or sexy people.

Jack needed to find what Jack always needed to find in moments of crisis. He began marching towards the city.

As he made his way towards the heart of Cardiff, he was passed by a number of locals. They laughed, they argued, they kissed or they listened to mp3 players. Some drove cars, others were on bicycles. Once in a blue moon, a motorcyclist roared past (Cardiff seemed to have fewer motorbikes per capita than anywhere else he'd visited). Normal people doing normal things with their normal lives.

These were the people that Jack and Torchwood protected, the vast majority of them never even realising they were being protected, let alone that there were Weevils, Rifts, giant space whales, alien guns, pendants, bombs or anything. It was a mark of how well Torchwood did their job that so few people died in inexplicable circumstances and asked questions. Even if they did, there was Toshiko, ready to create falsehoods and lies – not to mislead them, but again to protect them. Sometimes the truth was simply too awful and the concept of 'need to know' took on a whole new meaning.

Jack never stopped feeling responsible for his team – every one of them was there because he had found them, or they'd needed to find him. Now they were lost somewhere because of a battle that wasn't theirs.

Revenge for the future.

This was his little war, his and Bilis's, and whatever else was involved behind the scenes. Ianto, Gwen, Toshiko and Owen were, to Bilis, collateral damage, incidentals. To Jack they were his reason for being.

He would get them back. He would get them back safe and sound.

Because that was what good leaders did.

Because that was what Jack Harkness did.

He was walking along St Mary Street, Cardiff's old main street, before its famous shops had been usurped by the paved Queen Street during the 1970s. St Mary Street was now more famous for its clubs and bars and the network of alleys and arcades that branched off it.

To avoid a group of drunken youngsters, Jack took a sharp left into the tawdriness that was Wood Street. However beautiful Cardiff was – and he really did love his adopted city – this was the one blot on the landscape, a horrible, foreboding area of cheap shops, the grotty bus station and the main entrance to the Victorian façade of Cardiff's central railway station. For visitors to Cardiff, it wasn't an attractive greeting, and Jack had often wondered if he could fabricate some reason for Torchwood to blow it up so the council would have to rebuild it.

One to ask Idris Hopper one day, perhaps?

He was in Park Street now, adjoining the new Millennium Stadium that had swallowed up the old Cardiff Arms Park pitch, creating one huge super-venue, with its riverside views, cinema and sports shops.

One of his favourite parts of Cardiff, the street played host to the massive Ty Stadiwm tower, with its horizontal BT dish and mast on the very top.

As modern buildings went, in a city that juxtaposed the old and the new with pleasurable ease, Stadium House was one of Jack's favourites, mainly because – although it was a 'classic' 1970s structure – it had been beautifully refurbished (including the addition of the forty-two-foot mast) in the early part of the twenty-first century.

He entered the lobby, winking at Gerry, the security guard, and throwing some Swiss chocolate over to him. Each guard at each building had a weakness for something and Jack was friendly with them all. Chocolate was always the most popular bribe.

He took the service elevator and, moments later, he was nearly 255 feet above sea level, standing beside the 'dish' and looking down into the Millennium Stadium below. Thousands of empty seats surrounding a lush green pitch. If he closed his eyes, Jack could imagine the roar of the

Saturday afternoon crowd, smell the people, breathe in the beer, sweat and passion of the fans and players alike.

He looked up at the brightly lit antenna, thrusting upwards from the centre of the dish, illuminated to make it visible from miles away, casting numerous shadows of Jack across the rooftop.

The light. Something about the light…

Was it moving, was the light actual coalescing into something?

'Jack?'

'Greg?'

The shape of Greg's face, just an impression, seemed to swim in and out of existence, formed by the severe light from around the dish.

'Not long now, Jack, and it'll be over. The eternal battle for justice, for dominion. It's in the diary, Jack, it's all in the diary.'

And then, just for a few seconds, the lights went out. All over the city.

And the only illumination was provided by a crimson ribbon of Rift energy, stretching from the mast above him right across the city, and down to Cardiff Bay, where he could see it hovering just above where he knew the water tower sculpture was situated.

Within the Rift were thousands of dancing lights, and black blobs. Jack had witnessed Rift energy more times than anyone else on Earth, but he'd never seen so many pinpricks of light and dark inside it. Revenge for the Future? Jack began to understand.

Then the Rift energy was gone, and Cardiff came back to life.

'You can't do it, Owen! For God's sake, we've been here before. Light and Dark, two polar opposites. Try to stop one, you upset the balance of the Universe.'

Owen Harper just sighed at Jack, then reached out with his good hand and tapped the button on the control systems in the Boardroom. An image on the screen popped into life. It showed the Rift Manipulator as a cut-away diagram.

'Jack, listen to me. And if not me, listen to Gwen. Look at what we've achieved with the Rift. We can control it now, we could use it as a sort of gateway, pop in and out of places, get that alien tech we need to stop the bad guys.'

Jack looked at the others. 'Gwen?'

'I don't know, I can see the advantages, but I'm not convinced.'

'Tosh?'

'Jack, I have to say, I'm with Owen on this.'

'Only because you two discovered the light creatures. You might be under their spell for all we know.' Jack flicked the image off. 'I don't like it.'

'No, Jack, listen to us. There are things out there that could do marvellous things for this planet. We could, literally, change the world.'

'The mantra of the Torchwood Institute in London,' snarled Jack. 'Look where it got them.'

'They were stupid,' said Owen. 'They didn't have the foresight we have. Hell, they didn't have you as their moral compass.

But we have the chance here to do something really good. Tosh is right. The Rift could be our way to solving this planet's problems. Now we can control it.'

'Ianto?'

'I'm with Jack,' he said.

'Course you are,' said Owen. 'I mean, heaven forbid you might have an opinion of your own once in a while.'

'I do have opinions of my own. I just don't bother telling you what they are because you wouldn't like them.'

Gwen stood up. 'I'm sorry, but this question has been… consuming us this past couple of weeks. God knows what we're missing.'

Owen stabbed at the button again. 'Weevil sightings: none. Alien incursions: none. Dangerous bombs ready to blow Cardiff up: none. Sightings of Bilis Manger: none.'

'OK, Owen, you made your point.' Gwen switched the screen off again. 'But I'm still not letting this conversation continue.'

'Why not?'

'Because I have something to tell you. Something I hope won't result in me being shoved into a mortuary slab and all my personal belongings being stored in that garage for eternity.'

Jack frowned. 'You want to leave Torchwood?'

'You're being controlled by the Resurrection Boot and draining your life energy into Ianto?' That was Owen.

'You're proposing Andy Davidson, of Cardiff's finest, as a member of Torchwood?' asked Toshiko.

'She and Rhys are having a baby.' Ianto walked over and gave Gwen a hug.

'She told you?' said Jack, after a moment's pause.

177

'No,' said Ianto. 'I just keep my eyes open and my mouth closed.' He looked at Owen. 'You should try it.'

Gwen squeezed Ianto's hand. 'Thirteen weeks.'

Jack gave her a kiss, so did Toshiko.

Owen sat there, a smile on his face that he didn't feel.

And looked at Toshiko.

And instinctively thought of the box at his flat, in the empty, deactivated fridge that no one ever opened.

A box with a ring in it.

He sighed. He could never have kids. Not in his condition. And Toshiko – look at her face. The idea of a baby was thrilling her. How could he ask her to marry him? What was he thinking?

'Good one, Gwen,' he said. 'And tell Rhys that, too. I need to check on some specimens.'

He touched her hand as he walked out, and wondered if she flinched at his touch or whether, after all this time, it was still something he saw people do in his imagination.

He walked through the corridors and up towards the Hub.

A minute later, he stood looking at the base of the water tower. All it needed was some kind of energy boost, something that would ramp it up and open it permanently without destroying Earth.

It was a tall order, but he and Toshiko were so close to finding it.

So close to each other.

So close to marriage. To a life. To…

Oh God – that was it! Last time the Rift had opened, Abaddon had come through. Jack destroyed the Beast, time reversed as the Rift was sealed for good. No one died except Jack. And then he came back to life. It was Jack, something to do with him, with his unique energies.

And wasn't Jack always saying he'd happily sacrifice his immortality to be normal again?

What if they bled some of his life energies into the Rift – not a dangerous amount, but enough to see if it worked, however briefly. Then they could try and replicate those energies, because they'd have a sample of Jack's.

And Owen wondered what it would need to get some of his life energy.

And he suddenly thought of the pistol in the Autopsy Room.

No. No, that wasn't going to happen.

But an accident?

After all, accidents happened when you worked at Torchwood – he was the proof of that.

Was this him though? Or was Jack right? Were the light creatures in the Rift Energy affecting him? He was a doctor, committed to bringing life, not death.

And Tosh? What would she say?

He looked around the Hub and wondered where he was going next. He remembered something his mother had once said to him about power and corruption. And smiled.

This could be a whole new Torchwood.

Idris Hopper stood outside the tourist information entrance to Torchwood and frowned.

Who on Earth had put a huge metal strut across it and

padlocked it up? Jack? Closing Torchwood? Unlikely. Even at this time of night. But then, it was Jack. Anything was actually possible.

He shifted the record bag slung over his shoulder. The strap was beginning to dig into his neck a bit.

'Can I help you, sir?'

Idris turned.

Behind him was a short old man, dressed immaculately, a huge welcoming smile on his face. 'Are you looking for Mr Harkness?'

Idris thought about that – how likely was it that anyone around here knew Jack? Knew that this was the place to find him?

'I'm just trying to get in, but it seems to be locked up.'

The old man shrugged. 'Strange, isn't it? Torchwood is so rarely closed for business, but I saw Mr Harkness about half an hour ago, heading into the City Centre. I doubt he'll be long.' He pointed at the padlocked bar. 'Perhaps this is a new security measure. That Ianto Jones fellow can be such a stickler for detail.'

Idris shrugged. 'Yeah, guess so. Sorry, did you say "Torchwood"? What's that then? Is that the new name for the Tourist Board?' Idris pointed at the stylised red dragon symbol on the small sign that read *Croeso Cymru*. 'Never learned much Welsh at school. Wrong generation.'

The older Englishman just smiled. 'So few people around here seem proud of their rich heritage, Mr...?'

'Oh sorry.' Idris offered his hand. 'Hopper. Idris Hopper. I work for the Council. So, probably should know Welsh, but you'd be surprised how easy it is to get by with the odd *shwmae, os gwelwch yn dda, diolch, hwyl* or *nos da*!'

The old man nodded, understandingly. 'I have never spoken a word of Welsh either.'

Suddenly, Mermaid Quay was plunged into darkness, and there were surprised cries and yells from the people in the bars and restaurants.

Idris looked around, where had the old man gone?

Out of Idris's eyeline, something glowed a sort of purple in the sky – perhaps the columns of light that decorated the Oval Basin by the water tower were run independently.

Then life returned to the Bayside, and everyone breathed a sigh of relief.

As the bulb-lights around the jetties and decking spluttered back into life, Idris realised the old man was suddenly back again, uncomfortably close to his face.

Idris took a step back and was now pressed against the locked door.

'In fact,' the old man said as if nothing had happened, 'I shall be seeing Mr Harkness tomorrow. We have an... appointment. May I give him a message?'

Idris thought for a second and then smiled. 'God, you are a lifesaver.' He unslung his record bag and pulled out a sheaf of handwritten notes and a huge envelope. He then whipped out a pen and a set of Post-Its notes and scribbled a message down for Jack, attached them to the papers and shoved the pages into the envelope. He sealed the envelope, wrote Jack's name on the front, added 'By Hand Via Kindly Old Chum' in the corner and handed it to the man.

The old man smiled at the envelope. '"Kindly Old Chum" is a phrase I shall treasure, Mr Hopper.'

Idris offered his hand, but the man didn't take it. Instead he just bowed slightly.

'A pleasure to make your acquaintance, Mr Hopper. And good luck in Berlin.'

By the time Idris had registered that last comment, the man had vanished.

EIGHTEEN

It was a lovely morning. Simply delightful. No one in the world could have complained. The sun was out, the sky was blue with white fluffy clouds, and there was a tiny breeze in the air, but not enough to stop the general dress being T-shirts or halter tops.

Mums with kids in pushchairs and buggies, dads with older kids on their shoulders, teenagers and groups of pensioners all jostled on the roads of Tretarri, excited by this bizarre relaunch of a series of streets. Many arrived carrying the flyers that had been handed out around the city over the past twenty-four hours, detailing the clowns, magicians and street entertainers that would be present. Each flyer had a coupon that entitled the bearer to a can of drink each for their family (no more than four) at a discount rate. Light Lite it was called, guaranteed good for the kids.

The grand opening of the area had been at midday that morning. Jack had been there since 10 o'clock. Waiting. Watching. Wondering who, or what, would make a move.

The Wurlitzer had been the first thing to start up, sending out that irritating hurdy-gurdy music. Then the street performers had arrived, although Jack hadn't noticed where they'd come from. The houses? No doors were open.

Light Lite. He had picked up a discarded can earlier. The lights in the Rift last night. Greg talking about the Light and Dark. It all had to be connected somehow, he was sure of that, and all roads led to Tretarri.

The other thing that had occurred to him atop Stadium House the night before was that Tretarri might not be the casual annoyance he'd thought. Jack had been around for... well, centuries was not really an exaggeration. At around 150 years old, he'd seen a lot, remembered a lot (hell, he'd probably done a lot and what he hadn't done wasn't worth doing), and he was cross with himself for not recognising a trap when he saw one.

This was an elaborate ruse – had been ever since he'd first seen Tretarri back in 1902. Each time he'd come, the nausea had got stronger, a fact that hadn't really seemed important until now, but it was all leading somewhere, leading here. To now. Because Jack was an expert and could recognise a good party when he saw one. And this was the granddaddy of them all. All it needed was a host.

Where was Bilis Manger?

And where were his team? His friends?

Revenge for the Future.

What the hell was going to happen in the future?

Mind you, futures were fluid things. Time always was –

what you knew the future to be one day could be completely revoked when you next visited it. Like a river, ebbing back and forth, tiny ripples. The general shape of the big pond never changed but the detail of the ripples, the direction and mass, all that could be altered by the splash of a hand. Or the addition of a fish.

So, if his inability to access Tretarri was deliberate, and something was growing more powerful as time went by, there would have to be a point when the trap was sprung.

For that to happen, Jack would have to be given access to the streets.

He stared around him. The pavement-embedded uplighters were on, even though it was the middle of the day. The street lamps were on, too. Someone's carbon footprint wasn't making an indentation on their conscience. The lights in every house were on. But still no one was going in or out, the focus of the party atmosphere was external.

A clown was looking at him. Staring blankly, as if not quite seeing him. That was odd.

There was something about the way it was standing, head at a slight angle, the mouth beneath the big red painted lips.

God, no.

'Owen?'

Jack was walking across the road towards Tretarri, ignoring the nausea rising in his gut, fighting it down.

The clown he thought was Owen was caught up in a throng of children and, with a honk on a horn, it vanished, swept away by a sea of screaming, laughing kids.

Jack took a deep breath. Step by step.

One foot forward.

Owen. He had to get to Owen.

Another foot forward.

Jeez, he felt rank, could taste the bile.

If Owen was here, then maybe Toshiko, Gwen and Ianto were, too.

Another step.

Ianto!

The young man was standing outside 6 Coburg Street. Jack could see him. Staring away, Jack could only see one side of him. Could he catch his eye?

'Ianto,' he yelled.

A group of people turned and looked at Jack and then over at the man he was clearly yelling at, who gave no response. A little girl broke away from her family and ran to Ianto, pulling at his sleeve. Just enough to ease Ianto round to face Jack.

The right-hand side of his face was half clown make-up.

Why only half, Jack wondered. Owen was a complete clown (in so many ways, he thought wryly). Ianto was still in his suit. Why.

And Ianto in trouble, in possible pain, was enough for Jack. Enough to overcome the nausea, the sickness, the bile. For the first time in his life, he was capable of marching into Tretarri, past the crowds, the street performers, everyone. Until he reached Ianto.

He put a hand to his unpainted cheek.

'Ianto?'

'Jack?'

Jack turned. It was Bilis. At the doorway to number 6 Coburg Street.

'We should talk, I believe. And in here, we can.'

Jack frowned. 'Walk into my parlour?'

Bilis shrugged. 'Revenge for the Future?'

And Jack followed him in.

At the other end of the street party, wholly unaware of Jack, Ianto, Owen and Bilis, was Idris Hopper.

Why had he come? What had Jack stirred up in him that he felt the need to call in sick at work and head down here, to see if Tretarri really was worth the fuss Jack was making.

No sign of Jack though. 'Bloody Torchwood,' he muttered. 'I should know better.'

A man with a white face and stripy shirt approached him. A mime. He offered Idris a flower, but the Welshman shook his head and pushed past him with a weak smile.

A man in a suit was standing in front of a group of teenaged girls, who were giggling. He held up a pack of cards. A girl tapped one. The suited man shuffled the cards, then pocketed them, clapped his hands and pointed to a window in a house.

The girls whooped to see the card posted there.

The man, who never spoke, held a finger up, produced the pack again and offered them to a different girl. She selected a different card. The four of hearts. He showed everyone.

He got out a black marker and she wrote her name on it. Nikki, Idris noted.

He then reshuffled and this time gave her the pack, pointing at her handbag. She put the pack in the bag, and he gently took the bag from her and gave it a comical shake.

He then pretended to watch something invisible rise from her bag and everyone followed his eyeline, until it settled on the bag of the first girl to have picked a card.

He pointed at her bag, which she opened and, sure enough, found a card in there. The four of hearts. With 'Nikki' scrawled across it in black marker.

The applause and screams went up, and he bowed.

Idris carried on, past a stilt-walker and a female clown holding a bucket, which a few people dropped coins into. She never moved, never blinked.

He dropped a fifty pence piece in and walked on, not seeing the clown woman turn her head to watch him. Nor did he see her lower the bucket to the floor, and put a hand to the back of her trousers, as if expecting to find something tucked into the top.

Walking on down Wharf Street, Idris noticed that there was a statue in the middle of one of the connecting streets. He didn't remember that from the plans. Bronze, showing a Kabuki dancer, kimono, one leg tucked up, palms erect, a fan in each, the head at a slight angle, looking upwards. Only the slightest tremble made Idris realise this was in fact a painted human. He always found human statues a bit creepy. Not just because the lack of movement dehumanised them, but because it took a very special kind of person who could get satisfaction from standing stock still for so long.

He stared at the Kabuki for a moment. It didn't move again. He shrugged and turned away.

And therefore didn't see tiny spikes pop up at the top of each crease in the fans. Or the tucked leg return to the ground. Or the unsmiling head turn and watch him through jet black eyes, as it drew back one of the lethal fans, ready to throw it like a shuriken.

As Idris turned a corner and moved out of the Kabuki's view, she resumed her passive pose, the spikes retracting from the fans.

And the hurdy-gurdy music continued to sound, mixed with the laughter of happy families.

NINETEEN

When did it go wrong?

It was the question that had haunted Ianto Jones for about eighteen months. Now he believed he knew the answer – it was the day he'd spotted Gwen was expecting.

They had all been in the Hub Boardroom, and Jack was being an arse – well, a particularly arsey arse. And Owen had walked out.

Later that night, Owen had talked to Ianto about Jack. About the Hub. About Torchwood. And about the Rift. Dreams, ideas, plans. To use the Rift to help mankind.

All of which had seemed a good idea in principle, but not in practice.

'Look what happened last time we opened the Rift,' he'd said to Owen. But Owen had had an answer to that. Something about Jack, something about Jack's immortality being used to power the Rift ad infinitum.

'And this afternoon, just for a second, I did it. I accessed the Rift, I looked into it and realised its potential.'

'You did what?'

'Oh I closed it. God, it was barely a second, even Tosh's equipment barely registered it. You lot in the Boardroom certainly didn't.'

Ianto had been astonished. At first, he'd thought Owen was having a laugh, being the joker. But, as the evening had worn on, he'd realised Owen was serious.

Perhaps it was the accident, that moment when Owen's life had changed. Perhaps on that day, as Torchwood had pulled together to help him, perhaps there'd been some split moment in time. Owen had turned left with them. But what if, in Owen's head, he'd turned right. And that was what had led him to this. Telling Ianto that he was going to play God with Jack's help.

Except Ianto had known there was no way Jack would ever say yes.

He'd tried to persuade Owen, pleaded with him. To see sense. To talk to Jack. To let himself be talked out of this.

But Owen would have none of it and, during their increasingly heated argument, Ianto had realised what was causing it.

'It's OK for you. You've got Jack. Gwen has Rhys – God help us all – but what do I have? A knackered hand and no Tosh.'

Ianto had laughed. 'Tosh? You could have Tosh whenever you want. She's crazy about you.'

'Was.'

'Is!'

'Was. But now she's looking for more. And I'm not it.'

And Toshiko had chosen that moment to walk in.

Or, at least, to make her presence felt. In fact, Ianto had realised, she must have heard the whole thing.

She'd walked across the Hub from the water tower and straight up to Owen, pulling him to her and kissing him, hard. 'Is that proof enough, Owen?' she'd said as she eased away from him. 'I've always said that it's you, your heart, your soul I want.'

Ianto had coughed. 'If you'll excuse me, I have some washing up to do. I'll try not to clatter the cups too much.'

And he'd put Owen's master plan out of his mind and, instead, was happy that Tosh and Owen had finally found common ground with one another.

So how come he hadn't seen the changes over the next few months? Was it because he'd trusted his co-workers? His friends? Trusted them too much? Like Jack had. Was it because he'd never have believed Gwen could be corrupted? Owen, Toshiko even, they'd always had that potential, borrowing things from the safes and cabinets for their own ends, things that came through the Rift that could be used for their own hedonistic or selfish ends. But those were things that didn't really hurt anyone.

But then… then they'd taken it to a new level, and Gwen had been sucked into it. Alien tech that could revolutionise maternity practices. A quick call to the Prime Minister, Tosh using tech to disguise Owen's voice so it sounded like Jack's. How far could they go without seeing the moral implications?

Throughout time, mankind had created empires built around one or two people who believed what they were doing was right for the people, or fooled themselves into thinking that was so. Locking away their morality, their conscience, in a box. Driven by the rush of being able to do it rather than examining what 'it' was.

Owen and Tosh went down that slope so rapidly it was scary.

Everyone had that chance to turn left rather than right. Owen and Tosh had gone round the roundabout and traced a whole new route of personal morality that Ianto had never believed them capable of.

The Prime Minister had approved the exposure of Torchwood, and was then destroyed by his own policy of disclosure and open government. His administration fell in weeks, and Torchwood acceded to power in days.

Britain moved forward to a new age of enlightenment and industrial domination, aided by alien tech. China, the USSR, even America, they all wanted to get ahead of the game, but it was Britain, or the rapidly expanding Torchwood Empire, that held the reins of power.

Middle East peace in three weeks. Famine in Africa ended. Nuclear weapons dismantled. Star Wars satellites decommissioned. The world was made a safe, peaceful haven in eight months, with no loss of life.

Except one. One man.

They had betrayed him. They had sedated him and wired him up to the water tower, bleeding his energies into the Rift to open it safely, to monitor what came through, to cherry-pick what could, in their twisted minds, help the world.

Owen had realised early on that Jack Harkness could never be free again, that it was his role to serve with his limitless capacity for rejuvenation, and be the source of Torchwood's true power.

With Toshiko's help, Owen had trapped Jack, like an insect in amber, unconscious but alive, in a perpetual state of cryogenic suspension, feeding the Rift.

If Gwen had ever had any moral influence on Toshiko and Owen (and Ianto doubted it), once she had gone, they were free to do whatever they chose. Ultimate power – ultimate corruption. She had left Torchwood to have her baby. And that was when the creatures came though, breaching Toshiko's defences.

The Light and the Dark.

At first they'd thought they were just that, light fragments. It was Owen who'd hypothesised that they might be alive.

Ianto had tried again. After months away, he'd returned to the Hub. His own PDA, which he'd kept, just in case, monitoring Jack's vitals, had flared as the light creatures came through. He'd pleaded with Tosh and Owen to see how far they'd fallen. But they were almost evangelical. For Owen, this was a chance to contribute. For Toshiko, this was years of being downtrodden, forgotten and bullied coming to the surface in an explosion of bitterness and arrogance. All those years she'd been better, cleverer and smarter than the rest. Now she could prove it.

The Toshiko Sato and Owen Harper that Ianto had once known had gone for ever.

And when their eyes had briefly glowed with light, he'd sussed the truth. This really wasn't Toshiko and Owen. This was whatever they had unleashed from the Rift. It had been inside them, ever since that day Owen had looked into the Rift – passed into Toshiko via their first snog.

And Gwen? Poor silly Gwen, hormones in a mess with the pregnancy, either the Light had got into her in some way, or she'd just said yes to whatever the others wanted because it was easier for her.

No, that wasn't Gwen. There had to be more to it.

So Ianto had contacted Rhys and explained the situation. Rhys agreed. He'd never had much time for Jack, but he respected him. And he knew how strong the bond between his Gwen and Jack was. No way, Rhys thought, would Gwen have just approved this abuse of her friend.

So the Light had got into her, too.

Ianto had returned then to the Hub. One last chance. He had talked about what they'd achieved and what effect it was having on the population of Britain. The gap between wealth and poverty had never been wider; their Empire was founded on the oldest traditions in the world, he said – them and us.

Toshiko had insisted that would change. Gwen had tried to reason with him, saying she was his friend, but this was what the world needed.

In one last desperate move, Ianto had told them about the Light and the Dark. That he believed they were controlling his old friends.

And Toshiko had destroyed the future.

She'd destroyed the Hub.

A new Torchwood Institute had been constructed in the heart of Cardiff, at the very heart of the Rift – a massive office complex where the Castle had once stood, history demolished in days.

Then they moved the Rift Manipulator there, the whole water tower and Jack, encased in his glass prison. Lock, stock and barrel. The Hub was firestormed, destroying everything else, so no one else could ever access the past. The basements, the Morgue, the Vaults, over a century of information was lost for ever. Because this was a new Torchwood, burning brightly on the pyre of the old.

And Ianto had run, because he knew there was no way he'd survive the madness.

The last thing he'd seen as he left the Hub was light. Flickering lights in the air, dancing with one another. Or fighting. Black Light and White Light.

For weeks, Ianto had plotted and planned. The only way to put things right was to become everything he hated. He had to think like the enemy, act like the enemy. Ianto Jones had to become like Tosh and Owen. Like the light creatures from the Rift that possessed them.

He had to kill his old friends and bring down the Torchwood Empire.

It had taken them less than a year to take over the world. It would take less than two minutes to bring it crashing down.

Rhys Williams had phoned him. Gwen was in hospital. That had been Rhys's one condition. He'd made the plans Cardiff Council had, puppet authority that it now was, available to Ianto. He'd revealed the police routines, what was and wasn't protected. He'd known how to get about the city without being seen that day. And Ianto had taken the information and agreed that nothing would happen to Gwen or their baby boy. Hoping it was a promise he could keep.

Now he watched as Toshiko finished her address to the crowds, Owen at her side. He watched as they turned and entered the new Torchwood building.

197

Armed to the teeth, Ianto burst in after them.

For Ianto, it all happened in some kind of weird slow motion. The moment he saw the water tower there in the atrium, the glass panel in the floor beneath it, he dashed forward for one last look at Jack.

His Jack.

Trapped in perpetual agony, unwillingly destroying the world he'd spent so many years protecting. Loving. And turning down the chance to go home again, just to come back and help Earth.

He fired his pistol as soon as he saw Jack's body, screaming in anger, only dimly aware that he'd taken Owen out.

He didn't truly feel the pain as dozens of bullets ripped him apart, all his conscious mind was thinking of was how to get to Jack.

That somehow, in dying, Ianto could wake Jack up.

And Jack would stop the light creatures.

The last thing Ianto saw was his own blood obscuring the glass, hiding Jack's beautiful face from him.

And it was over.

In Bute Street, unnoticed by any of the passers-by, the clown paint seemed almost to move by itself on Ianto's face, dissipating into sparkles of light, which coalesced into a small starburst and shot off into the crowds.

And Ianto Jones staggered, grasping a lamp-post for support, and remembered the dream. He felt his torso, still in one piece.

Jack.

His love for Jack had brought him back, and now he had to find him. He had to find Jack.

Because he understood what was going on now, the struggle that was taking place in Cardiff. In Tretarri.

Revenge for the Future.

TWENTY

The room was dark, so dark. There was a table with a red chintz tablecloth on it. A teapot and two cups with saucers. A plate, some crustless sandwiches and two tiny cakes, iced, with chocolate sprinkles on top. The windows were covered by a heavy olive drape. In one corner was a leather armchair, and a table next to that.

A box on the table.

On the wall, photographs of Cardiff through the years.

'What do you want?'

Bilis Manger smiled, and pointed to the tea. 'A companion? To discuss life, the universe and the imminent destruction of this planet. Thanks to you.'

Bilis threw Idris Hopper's envelope across to him.

'One of your lesser minions delivered this to you last night. I intercepted it, but it's all nonsense.'

Jack tore open the envelope. It was a sheaf of papers, marked, 'TRANSLATION OF JACK'S (or whoever's) DIARY'. Typed beneath that, Jack read, 'Done extremely under protest by Idris Hopper who, God forbid he might actually have a life of his own, is actually bored by this. Oh, and Jack, you owe me £12.62 for lemon juice.'

Jack smiled and sifted through the translation. But it was just a series of notes about Victorian Cardiff, *circa* 1871.

'There's a note,' Bilis waved towards the envelope as he poured tea. 'Nice boy, by the way. One of your conquests? Looked the type. Thin. Breakable. Desperate for love and attention. Needing a father figure.' He passed the tea to Jack. 'Bit like your Ianto Jones, really.'

Jack ignored Bilis and shoved his hand into the envelope, tugging out the sticky Post-It that had got caught on the inside: '*Jack, mae'r boi'n siarad trwy'i din ac mae popeth fi'n ysgrifennu yma'n rwtsh llwyr. Mae'r dyddiadur dal gen i.*'

Jack pulled a face. His Welsh was rusty. 'Can you translate this? You know, being a man of the world?'

Bilis shrugged. 'As I told the lovely Mr Hopper last night, languages are not my speciality.' But he frowned. 'I assumed you'd be able to understand it though.'

Jack looked at the notes again, and then at Bilis. 'I get the gist. Thank you. For, you know, passing this on.'

'I don't like you, Captain, and I'm fairly sure you don't like me. But we are drawn together and, strange as it may seem, we are on the same side.'

'Really?'

'Oh yes, indeed.' Bilis sipped his tea. 'What do you know about consequences?'

'Lots. You?'

Bilis smiled. 'Yes. Many years ago, two demon beasts

fought for control of the Rift. Pwccm versus Abaddon. You are, of course, familiar with the latter.'

Jack just sniffed at the tea.

Bilis laughed. 'It's not poisoned, Jack. Really, how dull do you think I am?'

'What have you done with my team?'

'Honestly? Nothing. I needed to put them in a transient state, so they could dream the future.'

Jack stood up. 'I'm hearing words, Bilis. Sounds and nonsense. I'm not hearing explanations.'

Bilis sipped his tea again. 'You have lived for a long time, Jack. And by my reckoning, you will for a long time yet. You may even outdo me, who knows. I can't predict my own future, none of us can. But what I can do is see the possibilities. It's my gift. Or curse – that depends on one's point of view.'

'And you needed them why?'

'Because you are the future I'm concerned about Jack – and I can't read you. There, I've said it. You are a barrier to me, as Tretarri was to you until I was ready to let you in. Which today I did.'

Jack pointed outside. 'Why the party?'

'There's always a price to pay for freedom. I need to know how far you'll go to protect these ridiculous people and their corrupt world.'

'What is going on?'

'Consequences. Abaddon had a task, a significant place in the structure of things.'

'He destroyed lives.'

'He did that no more consciously than you and I breathe the air. It's what he did. He is... he was perfection. A purity so immaculate, so delicate because your evil was his good. He did what he did to survive. And, to protect.' Bilis poured more tea. 'What you fail to grasp, Jack Harkness, is the consequences of your actions. The people of this era, this time, they irradiate their crops with insecticides, because the tiny creatures they hate destroy their crops. When they destroy the insects, the things the insects feed on then live, flourish and grow stronger. With no natural predators, they mutate.'

Jack moved to pull the drapes open, to let some light in.

Bilis clicked his fingers, and suddenly Jack wasn't facing the window, he was facing the opposite wall. Angrily he turned around again.

Bilis just smiled at him, a teacher addressing a slightly dim pupil. 'You have to understand, everything in this house is mine to control, even you. You will listen to me because, out there, I can't control anything, but in here we can talk. We are... protected.'

He pointed to the box on the table.

'The essence of what I am here to protect. It was dying, spent and exhausted, trying to fight a battle it could no longer win because someone had taken away its insects. Or its demons, to use your vernacular, gauche as it is.'

Jack sat in the armchair and tried to open the box.

'Jack?'

'Greg?'

The apparition of Greg Bishop was facing him and, in

the room, able to see it clearly, he realised the outline of his old friend and lover was constructed from tiny lights.

'Natural halogens,' Bilis said. 'Back in 1941, I needed a vessel to keep them from dying, to give them something to focus upon, to construct a new existence around. Mr Bishop had the diary in his hands, he became their vessel.' He clapped his hands. 'Lemon juice! Of course, Mr Hopper has the diary, and you asked him to find out what it said. I never managed that, you see.'

Bilis reached for the papers Idris had given Jack, flicked through them, and angrily tossed them to the floor. He swung around to Jack, suddenly angry, light blazing literally in his eyes. 'I need that diary, Jack. It contains the solution.'

'It contains words, Bilis. That's all. You had it when you gave it to Tilda Brennan.'

'No, you fool. I never had it. The Torchwood Institute had it, they defiled a grave to acquire it, because they wanted to release what was in it. That's why it took Greg Bishop here. I didn't do that, Abaddon didn't do that. Greg's death is entirely on your conscience because none of this need have happened if you hadn't destroyed Abaddon.'

'I destroyed Abaddon this year. What happened to Greg was in 1941.'

'Revenge for the future! It was a message. Contained in the ink the diary was written in. It is not in the words, it's in the ink. I gave the diary to a trustworthy man who owned the area where the Lords fought for control of the Rift, where my Lord Abaddon faked defeat so he could prepare and gain strength. This place, Tretarri.'

Jack stood again. 'So let me get this straight. A fight in the nineteenth century between two creatures for supremacy over the Rift. Abaddon was one of those. And he apparently lost. You gave some guy the secret to releasing Rift energies that foretold the future and, when Torchwood got in the way, you needed me to sort it out. By lying, deceiving and killing my friends, you got me here, today, in the hope that somehow I'd do what? Bring Abaddon back?'

Bilis shook his head. 'Abaddon was the Devourer. His role in life, in eternity, was to destroy the Darkness. You stopped that.'

'He killed hundreds.'

'They were irrelevant!' Bilis was almost shouting now. 'Insignificant insects, food to keep him sated so he could achieve the apotheosis of his mission. To protect the Rift from the Dark.'

And Jack remembered the lights he'd seen in the Rift storm the previous night. Blobs of light and dark.

'They live in the Rift, Jack. Beings of pure halogen, elements of intelligence, at war for millennia. Abaddon was protecting the Light from the invasion of the Dark. And you stopped it.'

Jack thought about this. 'Where is the Light now, other than here creating images of Greg Bishop?'

Greg's ghostly form turned to Jack. 'I saw the future, Jack. I saw all those potential ifs, maybes and buts. The Dark will be released by your team in the future. Corrupting your people until they build an empire of Darkness over this world, so they can feed. I'm sorry, Jack, I couldn't intervene, the Light is so weak. It needs hosts, otherwise it will die. And the Dark will live.'

'And this is in the future?'

'The near future.'

Bilis stood between them. 'That is why I took your team out of the action, Jack. While I keep them suppressed, the corruption cannot occur.' He pointed to the box on the table. 'It's a prison, Jack. The Light and the Dark need to be drawn into it, to continue their eternal battle in a prison. The Light is willing to make the sacrifice to save this world, to save the Rift. Are you?'

Jack looked at Bilis. At Greg.

'No. No, I'm not. Because I don't believe a word you say.'

Ianto was sitting on the pavement, the crowds milling around him, his head in his hands.

A mime tried to reach down and pull him up and, as Ianto looked up to refuse, the mime simply flickered, like a faulty light.

The effect on the mime was devastating. He hit the ground with a colossal smack, and Ianto was at his side in a moment.

Events like this – always a St John Ambulance man somewhere to hand.

'Help,' he called out.

Then he frowned. The mime simply melted away in his hand, and in his place was a bunch of tiny spots of bright light. Like the ones that had occupied him when Bilis had held him.

Ianto backed away, and careered into a man who'd been watching him.

'Did I just see what I thought I saw?' asked the man.

Ianto pulled himself together, Torchwood training taking over. 'Not sure what you mean, sir.'

The man looked at him and smiled. 'You have to be Ianto Jones. The suit, the neatness.' He paused, then smiled. 'Jack's fond of you. My name is Idris.'

Ianto knew immediately who he was talking to. 'From the Council?' How lame did that sound?

Idris laughed. 'You could say that. I came looking for Jack.'

'Not seen him,' Ianto said, more truthfully than he'd have liked. The memory of that dream was still raw.

A hand touched his shoulder.

'Good to see you back in the land of the living, Ianto,' said Jack. 'Hi there, Idris. Good job on the paperwork. Where's the diary?'

Idris smiled at Jack. 'In my bag. Along with...' He brought out another set of papers with a flourish. 'The real translation!'

Jack nodded. 'Took a gamble that my reading Welsh was better than my spoken Welsh. And you were right – it fooled Bilis long enough. Thank you.'

Ianto suddenly hugged Jack, tightly, and didn't let go. He whispered into Jack's ear. 'What does "Revenge for the Future" mean to you?'

'If I knew that, I'd be a happier man. Another thing I'd like to understand.'

'Yes?'

'That.'

Jack was pointing at the people in the street. Clowns, magicians, tricksters – and all the general public who had come to see them. All standing watching the three men. Their eyes gone, replaced by burning fierce light.

Except five people to one side. A mum, dad and child, an old lady and the Kabuki living statue performer Idris had seen earlier.

Their eyes were gone, too, but replaced by a dark blackness. No light – the very opposite of light – and from within came something darker than the most powerful black hole.

'Tosh?'

Ianto looked at Jack and then at the Kabuki.

And under the make-up and clothes, yes, it was Toshiko.

The light-embodied others turned to look at the five newcomers.

'This isn't going to be good,' muttered Jack.

He grabbed Ianto and Idris and bustled them into number 6 Coburg Street.

In the room, the outside still cut off by the olive drapes, Bilis and the shimmering form of Greg waited.

Jack crossed to the window. 'Let's shed a little light, shall we?' He threw open the drapes and turned to Bilis.

'Well?' said the old man.

'All right, so maybe there's some truth in what you told me, Bilis. What do we need to do?'

'I don't know,' he said simply.

'What?' shouted Ianto.

Bilis sighed. 'This is your fault. All of you. I protected the Light. Abaddon protected the Light. The diary please, Mr Hopper.'

Idris looked to Jack, who nodded. He passed the book to the old man.

'You read it I assume. Any clues?'

'To what?'

'Idris, what did it say?' asked Jack quietly.

And Idris told them what Gideon ap Tarri had seen, how Bilis had given him the diary and pen and instructed him to have it buried with him. 'The last thing he said was he was going to try and escape from the Scottish Torchwood guy. That was it.'

Bilis was running his hands over the diary. 'Yes, this is it. The protection is still here.' He looked at Greg Bishop's ghostly form. 'Thank you.'

Before Jack could say anything, Bilis had opened the book, and Greg's form immediately dissipated. A blur of light shot into the pages of the book, briefly forming written words that soon faded.

Bilis looked at Jack, an expression of pity on his otherwise serene face. 'He died in 1941, Jack. They just kept his essence alive. If it makes you feel any better, you chose the right man to love. He was, in every way, a good man.'

Ianto was looking at Jack, but the older man was ignoring him.

'What has happened to Tosh?'

Holding the book to his chest, Bilis closed his eyes. When he opened them again, he looked almost sympathetic. 'I'm so sorry,' he said. 'She is lost to the Dark.'

'Not on my watch she isn't,' Jack said.

Outside, the assembled crowds, both white-eyed and dark-eyed, took a step in unison towards the house.

'OK – that's creepy,' Ianto said.

'Saw that in a Michael Jackson video once,' said Idris. 'They were zombies, too.'

'Bilis?'

'It's the age-old fight, Jack. Evil versus… Well, there's such a grey area between good and evil really isn't there? One man's demon is another man's god.'

'Jack,' Ianto grabbed his sleeve. 'I had a dream.'

'Oh God, it's Martin Luther King,' Idris muttered.

'Is this the time, Ianto?' Jack wondered.

'Yes, Jack, it is. Light versus Dark. The lights. There were lights in the Rift storm.'

Jack recalled what he'd seen on top of Ty Stadiwm the night before. He was getting cross, because it kind of tied in with what Bilis had been saying, and Jack's biggest fear right now was that Bilis was right and this was all a consequence of what he'd done months ago.

He looked Bilis in the eye. 'To hell with consequences, Bilis. If I stopped every time I opted to save human lives, stopped to think about who I was saving or what I was saving them from, I'd never move. Never decide. Be caught with an endless stream of possibilities, probabilities and maybes ahead of me.'

'Welcome to my life, Jack,' Bilis said.

'I will not apologise for destroying Abaddon. I will not apologise for the fact that by destroying him we closed the Rift and brought everyone back to life. Some of those people are probably standing out there today. I did not fail them then, and I'm damned if I will do it now.'

Bilis took a breath. 'The Light and the Dark, Jack. We don't need to imprison them both! We can split them up, trap the Dark in the box I showed you, and release the Light into the Rift. From there, they will return down below where they belong, keeping Pwccm imprisoned for eternity. Because, however evil you believe my Lord to have been, you do not want Pwccm released in his stead. And that's what you disturbed, Jack. In destroying Abaddon, the other Beast and his Dark warriors were able to imprison the Light. I saved some of them, kept them in the box. We can do a swap, because Pwccm has been foolish enough to send his soldiers into this dimension to fight the Light.'

'You mean, we're just caught up in a battle between alien light creatures from another dimension? That this has nothing to do with us?' Ianto shook his head. 'Just another day at Torchwood then. So… where does this Revenge for the Future thing come in?'

Bilis shrugged. 'I'm not sure – it was what the Light said. It's why Greg Bishop said it when possessed by them. It's why it's in the diary, which is what can keep the Light alive – the ink it made from their life essences.'

'OK.' Jack took a deep breath. 'Light: they need to be back in your diary for safekeeping. Dark, they need to go into the prison box. Neither actually live naturally in the Rift energy, but both have used it as a mode of crossing the dimensions. On the mark so far?'

Bilis nodded.

'So what actually released them. Here and now?'

'I doubt they are from the here and now,' said Bilis.

'Revenge. For the Future. Something we did – I did? – in the future will release them? I release the Dark light, and the Light light want revenge on me for that?'

'Hence the trap, Jack,' Bilis stepped towards him. 'You had to be old enough, wise enough to be prepared. I can't tell you what the journey you are going to embark upon will show you. I only see possible futures and none I've seen explains the Dark's release. But the Light wanted you here for a reason.'

'He could be lying,' Ianto said.

'Ya think?' Jack sighed. 'But whatever it is, I need to know. Ianto, Idris, if this goes wrong, I want Bilis, bullet, back of the head before he can vanish.' He looked at Bilis. 'Got that?'

'Kill him?' Idris was horrified.

'Um, problem Jack. I don't have a gun any more.' Ianto smiled sheepishly. 'Sorry.'

Bilis produced Ianto's pistol out of thin air and placed it in Ianto's palm. He smiled and put his hands round Jack's clenched fists. 'A show of faith. I need the Light saved and the Dark imprisoned. Or I will have failed. And I never fail.'

'Well, except with Abaddon,' Ianto said.

'Not helping, Ianto,' Jack said.

'Sorry.'

'Look at me, Jack.' Bilis's face filled Jack Harkness's field of vision.

Jack gasped as the old man's eyes flared with the halogen brilliance of the Light.

And it poured into Jack's own eyes.

TWENTY-ONE

Jack Harkness knew every nook and cranny of the Torchwood Hub in Cardiff. At least, that's what he'd always thought, but clearly there were bits he wasn't that good on because somehow he was lost.

The corridors had been hollowed out of the solid rock beneath Cardiff Bay a century or so earlier, but had fallen into disrepair between the wars. Only a few direct routes to the basement rooms were regularly kept up to date. Recently, his team had opened a few more up – some of which had been done while he'd been away all those months ago.

Hell, they'd even built a new Boardroom! How cool was that?

How cool it'd be if he could get there now. It was defendable.

But here in these corridors with their junctions, shadows, low ceilings and sudden maze-like twists and turns, he felt dead vulnerable and hopelessly lost. He was running, probably for his life.

And who from?

He'd been in the Hub, talking to Gwen, when Ianto had called him on his cell phone. Mobile. Whatever.

'Where the hell are you today?'

'Jack – you gotta get out of there,' Ianto had yelled, loud enough that the others had heard him.

Jack gave Owen and Gwen an 'oh my god, has he been drinking' look and told Ianto to calm down.

'Who's with you?'

'Owen and Gwen. Tosh is down in the Boardroom. Oh, and the Weevils are in the Vaults, as normal. I think that's it. You OK?'

'Get. Out. Jack. Now!'

Suddenly the phone reception screeched and went dead. Jack nearly dropped his phone.

Gwen shot a look at Owen. 'I'll go find Ianto,' she said and, before Jack could stop her, she was gone.

Except for that brief moment when she stopped by the rolling door and looked back at him.

Just for a second.

One look.

By the time the door had rolled closed behind her, Jack had the Webley out and ready.

And then he had started running.

Now he was lost in the corridors. He slowed to a halt, pausing while he tried to work out where he was, tried to come up with a plan.

He felt the hard steel of a pistol on the back of his head.

'Owen? What exactly is going on?'

'Don't move, Jack. I'm sorry. God, I'm really, really sorry, but you don't understand what we're doing here.'

'Too damn right I don't.'

'Please, Jack.'

That was Toshiko. So she was in on it, too. Whatever 'it' was.

'Another coup, Owen? This is getting really tired.'

'Jack, you've got to understand, we've found a way to help the world.'

'I thought we were already doing that.'

Toshiko came into view. 'No, we mean really help it. Change it. Make everything better. Instead of just squirreling everything away, we could actually use it to better mankind.'

Jack just shrugged. 'Heard that before, guys. It's what brought down the Institute in London. I thought we were better than that.'

Owen nodded, understanding Jack's concerns. 'And that's why we need you. Our moral compass. They never had that. They never had you.'

'And what do I need to do for your brave new world, Owen? What's the price? Cos I've been around, you know. I realise there's always a price.'

Owen and Toshiko glanced at one another.

'And Gwen?' Jack continued. 'Is she OK with this?'

'Gwen's… undecided, if I'm being honest,' said Toshiko.

'Honesty, well that's good. Keep with the honesty programme, Tosh, and tell me what you need me for. Cos I have a feeling I'm not gonna like it.'

'You're right, Jack,' Owen said, in a suddenly calm and strong voice. 'You're not.'

217

Jack saw his eyes. Solid black, like the heart of a black hole had consumed him from inside. He looked at Toshiko. She was the same.

'Shit,' said Jack, and Owen shot him dead, straight through the forehead.

When Jack awoke, he couldn't move.

He opened his eyes, but he was in an opaque nothingness, although it was solid, he was sure of that. He tried moving. Nope, held rigid, and all he could do was look slightly left or right with his eyes. Nothing else moved, although he could feel his body.

So he was trapped, encased in something that held him still.

He became aware of tiny pinpricks on his skin, like a million tiny needles painlessly pressing against him.

After more than 150 years, Jack knew his own body, he knew every millimetre of skin and muscle and tissue and how it should feel at any given moment. And whatever this was, it was wrong.

Something loomed into view above him, misshapen, distorted. It spoke, the sound distorting through whatever it was that held him there. He realised it was Owen Harper, his eyes still consumed by the black.

'Jack,' he was saying. 'Not sure if you can hear me, but every few hours, you'll suffocate. And then come back to life.'

Wasn't the first time that trick had been tried, Jack thought ruefully. But why?

'And when that happens, the energies your body gives off

will enable us to open the Rift and, more importantly, control it. We are going to use the Rift to build a new Torchwood Empire and make Earth a better home for everything trapped upon it.'

Interesting use of words. So whatever was inhabiting the others, it was trapped here.

Jack noted to himself that he'd automatically dismissed the notion that Toshiko and Owen and probably Gwen were doing this voluntarily. Something had taken them over.

Good. At least he wasn't being betrayed by his team.

He realised that the pinpricks were tiny wires into his skin, and that this had been worked out meticulously. And no matter how good Toshiko and Owen were, bless 'em, they couldn't have achieved this with just their technological savvy.

Aliens? Rift aliens? Something else?

It didn't matter. He was trapped, and encased in some kind of holding prison, unable to move and would, eternally, be living and dying and powering the aliens and their plans.

Great.

There was nothing he could do. Except wait for help from Ianto or someone else.

Jack smiled. Because he knew that Ianto would find a way. Because he was Ianto.

A long time passed. A lot of deaths and rebirths. Jack had no idea of time or space any longer – it was all he could do to keep sane.

Then, one day, a series of cracks appeared in the compound that held him.

He heard lots of noise, gunfire perhaps, and clearly some bullets had hit the thing he was in.

His vision clouded with scarlet. Had he been shot? No, no someone else had, directly above him, on the surface of the compound.

He knew then that Ianto was dead. Somewhere inside his head he felt something sever and die.

And he understood. Ianto had got himself shot, somewhere above him, deliberately. Knowing that his sacrifice was the only way to break the compound holding Jack. The crimson running across his vision and down tiny splinters in the compound towards him was Ianto's blood.

Jack felt himself tense. Anger, hurt, pain, betrayal, fury. All of those came together as his cheek felt a drop of Ianto's blood hit it.

Summoning every primal ounce of strength in him, Jack Harkness screamed in rage and pushed himself up, ignoring the searing pain as the compound shattered and sliced into him, ignoring the awful sensation of pure light hitting his eyes, blinking away the brightness and the blood.

He was standing there, threads of wiring torn away from his body, facing a group of armed guards, suited workers and Toshiko, her eyes now black, her face snarling.

'Kill him,' she screamed.

As if in slow motion, the guards raised their automatic weapons, but Jack was driven by something more powerful than good sense or logic.

He was driven by the death of Ianto Jones.

He reached forward and snatched a gun from a guard,

swinging round, firing as he did so, not giving a damn who died as the spray of bullets went out. This wasn't a time to care, this was a time for revenge. Revenge for the future of Earth, a future that was going to be destroyed if the aliens weren't stopped.

He watched as a couple of guards fell astonished before him, grabbing another weapon and firing it equally indiscriminately, determined to ignore the bullets that were now peppering him. Without him, the alien plan probably couldn't work. But he was going to take as much down with him as he could, just in case.

He saw Tosh suddenly gasp and a black... cloud erupted from her mouth, nose and eyes, as whatever alien was there fled her. Dark light – somehow he knew that was the phrase. On the ground at her feet, Owen's body, already dead, convulsed as the aliens left that too.

Jack dropped to the ground, as the bullets from the remaining guards did their work. He let himself roll back, taking the last armed guard down with him, and took in the water tower behind him, the exposed Rift Manipulator flashing away, as its power was disrupted.

Summoning the very last vestiges of life within him, Jack fired straight into it, and with a series of explosions, the Manipulator exploded.

He was aware, as if hearing it from a million miles away, of the huge rumble. Aware of screaming people running out of whatever building they were in, ignoring the dead and wounded around them. Aware of the Dark combining and racing towards him.

221

Jack crawled over to the water tower. He realised that Toshiko was there with him, tears flowing down her cheeks. As they hit the base of the tower together, Jack shoved his hand into the burning Manipulator, ignoring the pain as his finger burned and blistered, melted flesh and bone.

He screamed as Toshiko grabbed him, held him, sobbing her apologies.

'Not your fault,' he gasped, every breath pure agony.

'Theirs.'

And they both watched as the Dark sped towards them.

And Jack wrenched everything out of the Manipulator.

The staff at St Helen's Hospital were in panic. All the power in the hospital had cut out and no one knew why. Then they felt the ground shake, as windows exploded and a hundred car alarms in the car park roared into life.

Gwen Williams convulsed as the Torchwood equipment designed to extract the baby from within her failed.

Unseen by the doctors and nurses, a tiny cloud of Dark light emerged from Gwen's mouth as she screamed. It vanished immediately in a silent explosion, dying before it could find a new host.

A couple of nurses went into professional overdrive, immediately preparing Gwen for a caesarean.

Rhys was beside her.

An hour later, Rhys Williams held Geraint Williams Junior in his arms, singing Welsh rugby songs to him.

Gwen, smiling and exhausted, had just come round.

'What happened, Rhys?' she asked. 'I can't remember much

of anything. Like a fog has been lifted.'

Rhys took her hand. 'There was an explosion, love, at the heart of Cardiff. Terrible – a whole section of the city has gone, there's just a crater.'

And Gwen looked at him as memories flooded back.

She cried for half an hour. The nurses took the baby to the nursery while Rhys looked after his wife.

Every so often, she'd say, 'I didn't know what I was doing or thinking,' and 'I let them control me,' and 'I'm so sorry,' but Rhys didn't care. He had his wife back and safe and alive and well and a perfectly healthy baby.

He did though have things to say to her when she was calmer. Two things in fact.

First that, lovely as Geraint was as a first name, he thought Jack Ianto Geraint Williams was a better choice. Then he said something she'd never forget.

'Torchwood, as we knew it, has gone, love. Jack, Ianto, Owen and Toshiko, gone. But there still needs to be a Torchwood of sorts. Someone's got to carry on doing what you lot did.

'So you and me, yeah? Together. And we'll find more people: new Tosh, new Owen. And we'll make this place safe again. Somewhere safe for the baby to grow up.'

And Gwen hugged him harder than ever before.

TWENTY-TWO

The bucket hit the ground with a loud crash, and coins spilled everywhere over the road.

Gwen Cooper awoke from whatever dream she'd had with a gasp.

She could see people around her, clown faces on all of them. Not just the street performers but what appeared to be normal members of the public. Bits of the last few hours juddered into her mind, and she remembered that the plan was to lure people here, to get the Light inside them... for safekeeping. Just a race of alien life forms that needed temporary hosting, until their own habitat became available again.

Something about a diary. And Bilis Manger. He was their... friend?

And that awful future world where she'd been infected by Dark light... and Torchwood had tried to dominate Earth and been destroyed.

'Jack!' Gwen yelled at the top of her voice.

Everyone else in the street turned and looked at her.

As one, they marched towards her, card players throwing cards at cars and doors where they stuck, a mime imitating her every move as she made it.

And the people, the average normal people, their movements jerky as if they were trying not to let themselves be moved along by whatever it was that made their eyes shine.

That was all scary enough. But it was nothing to the dozen or so standing to one side, watching her like the others but through eyes that were pitch black, dead almost.

And Gwen knew that Dark light, knew it from the vision of the future. It had been inside her, made her turn away from Jack, from Torchwood and very nearly from Rhys and her baby.

Baby. My God, would she and Rhys have kids one day?

Yes. Yes they would. Yes, she was going to get married, and Torchwood would survive, and there was no way she'd let Owen and Toshiko fall to this Dark light, whatever it was. Because the future was not cast in stone, it was malleable, fluid.

Somehow, they'd been given a chance to make sure this didn't happen. That's why Bilis had put the Light inside her. A forewarning.

She had to find Owen and Toshiko, warn them and…

Oh.

She looked again at the Dark light people. The clown to the left. The golden statue woman in the kimono.

Shit.

The clown was Owen.

The statue was Toshiko.

Was it too late?

She tried to sidestep the crowd, but they seemed to anticipate her every move… But they weren't attacking her, they were actually making her walk back down the street, towards the place where she and Ianto had met Bilis.

Where he had put the Light inside her.

Oh my God, they weren't threatening her, they were keeping her apart from the Dark light group. From Owen and Toshiko.

She didn't need to go forward, she needed to go where they were herding her.

And again, as she turned and ran, not entirely sure where she was going, she yelled out, really, really loudly, 'Jack!'

In 6 Coburg Street, Jack was sitting in the armchair, and Ianto was crouching down beside him.

Bilis Manger stood by the window, arms behind his back, a gun pressed against his head by Idris Hopper. Well, not so much pressed as jabbing him like an insect, thanks to Idris's shaking hands. Holding a gun wasn't something the average Secretary to the Mayor's Office did on a daily basis.

'Jack!'

They all heard Gwen's voice from outside.

Jack looked up at Ianto. 'Let her in.' He then nodded to Idris, who gratefully lowered the gun and handed it over to Jack.

A second later, Ianto came back into the room, with Gwen close behind him.

She looked about her. 'Nice place you have here, Bilis. Decorate it yourself?'.

Jack and Idris exchanged confused looks.

'Ah,' Bilis said. 'Perception filters. Useful things, I'm sure you'll agree.'

He clicked his fingers and they were inside a shop. Bilis's clock shop. A Stitch in Time. Outside, people were walking down a Cardiff arcade, staring at other shops.

He clicked his fingers a second time, and the room became Coburg Street again, although clearly this was a surprise to Gwen.

'The place takes on an appearance that seems familiar. It shows you an environment where you might expect to find me. Gwen, here, associates me with clocks, as did Ms Sato. Hence the shop we met in once before. The rest of you expected to see the insides of an old Victorian two-up two-down, and that's what you got.' He smiled at Jack. 'Or did you see something else?'

Jack smiled back. 'That'd be telling.'

Bilis nodded. 'We have so much in common, you and I. A shame we find ourselves on opposing sides. Nine times out of ten.'

'Jack,' Gwen cut across them. 'The people outside, they're inhabited by Rift aliens, the—'

'Light, yeah we know,' Ianto finished. 'Providing hosts until we can get them home.'

'Then we got it all wrong,' Gwen said. She turned and

pointed at Bilis. 'He's not the enemy.'

'This time.' Bilis bowed. 'Well, I'm just saying what you're all thinking.'

'We have to get Tosh and Owen back,' said Jack. 'I have a plan, but I need them at the Hub.'

'A plan?' asked Bilis. 'Perhaps you would care to share your plan, Captain?'

'Not yet.' He looked at Idris. 'You in?'

Idris was horrified to hear his own voice reply, 'God, yeah.'

'Good. Bilis, you now have the book, the diary. That should be able to store the light creatures, if they trust you enough to go back into it.'

'Correct.'

'Then why'd you give it away to start with?' asked Ianto.

And for the first time, Bilis's demeanour lost its benign, slightly patronising look.

'The Light had a job to do, helping Abaddon. By keeping the diary away from the agents of the Dark and Pwccm, I ensured that the Light could not be harmed. Once Abaddon was destroyed, the Light were vulnerable, so I needed to get the diary back and return them... to where they belong. To survive. To protect this planet in my Lord's absence.'

'Good,' Jack said, dismissing Bilis's evangelical tirade as swiftly as possible. 'Now get out there and do it. Ianto, go with him.'

They left with the diary.

Jack turned to Gwen. 'You saw the future?'

'Did you believe it?'

Jack shrugged. 'Not really. It's just a possibility.'

'Jack, I'm so sorry. We did—'

Jack held up a hand. 'No. No you didn't, and that's the point. The light creatures were telling us what could happen if the balance between them isn't restored. Presumably it's how they communicate. Nice, if a bit melodramatic. Now, I think we can open the Rift and draw the Dark light creatures into it, but we need a booster. The Rift Manipulator at the Hub isn't enough. It needs something to fine tune them, as it were.'

Idris moved forward. 'There's always—'

But Jack cut him off. 'Hang on. Gwen, what if we let them swamp someone?'

'That'd be suicide.'

'Excuse me,' Idris tried again. 'But I know of a point where—'

Gwen waved him quiet and looked back at Jack. 'I mean it, there is no way we're letting you take on that responsibility.'

'It's my choice, Gwen, don't forget that.'

The door to the room crashed open. It was a breathless Ianto. 'Got a little problem.'

TWENTY-THREE

Outside the house, Jack and Gwen stared at Ianto's 'little problem'.

The Light had left the people. Bilis triumphantly clutched the diary to his heart. 'I just need to use the Rift energy to return them home,' he murmured.

'Sure you do,' said Jack. 'Doesn't help us with that!'

Everyone on the street now looked as Toshiko did. Eyes full of Dark light stared at the Torchwood group.

'Did you do this?' Gwen asked Bilis.

'No,' said Ianto. 'I reckon he was as surprised as I was.'

Jack grabbed Bilis, swung him round. 'So, you gonna disappear on us or help?'

Bilis just looked serenely up at him. 'Help, of course. I can't release the Light if the Dark is still at large. We need to imprison the Dark in the box.'

'Via Rift energy,' Jack finished. 'Got it.'

A clown stepped forward. Jack realised it was a disguised Owen.

The clown pointed at the diary.

Jack nodded. 'Yeah, we got the point. You want the little Light guys. We don't want you to have the little Light guys. Eternal war, across the dimensions, yadda yadda yadda. Tough.'

He turned away from Owen.

'Gwen,' he hissed. 'What broke Bilis's little spell on you?'

'Remembering the future,' she replied.

'But Ms Cooper was infected by the Light,' Bilis insisted. 'It is the Dark that controls these people.'

'Same principle must work though,' said Ianto. 'You put the Light in us, those two must have lost it, and that let the Dark in. How?'

Bilis shrugged. 'Perhaps, in some tiny gap between expelling the Light back into me and before wakefulness, the Dark took hold.'

'Why not me or Jack?' Gwen looked at the diary. 'It's something to do with that, isn't it?'

'No,' said Bilis. 'I think it's the prison box. I used the very last of the Light on the Captain here, the prison is empty of everything now. Perhaps with nothing to link either Dark or Light to the prison, it all had to go somewhere. So the Dark took hosts, just as the Light had.'

Idris raised his hand, like a school kid.

'What?'

'You need something to focus this Rift energy you keep talking about, right? The tallest building in Cardiff has a great big aerial on top of it. Can't you use that?'

232

Jack hugged Idris. 'Stadium House! Idris, you're a genius!' He turned to Bilis. 'I can stop this. We boost the power to the aerial, tune it to the Rift frequency. That high up, the Dark light will flock to it. Once captured, we drain it back via the Manipulator in our Hub and straight into your prison box. Job One done. Job Two, you're responsible for. You have to get your Light out of the diary and into the ground or whatever. You need Rift energy for that, but we can't risk the Dark and Light combining. So you do that when we've dealt with the Dark, right?'

Bilis understood. 'I need to be here to do that.'

'You need to be where I tell you,' snapped Jack. 'And for now that's at the Hub. Ianto will show you how to rig your prison box into the water tower.'

'He will?'

'I will?'

'Yeah.'

'No, Jack. I haven't got a clue. You need Tosh or Owen or both for that. Sorry.'

Jack deflated slightly.

'How did you get the Light into Jack and everyone?' Idris asked Bilis.

'I absorbed it myself, then spread it into them. It's easy, the Light likes new hosts.'

'So,' Idris said slowly, 'if we could drain Owen and Tosh of their Dark and then re-host it, they'd be free, yes?'

Bilis nodded. 'I am able to play host to the Dark. I am strong enough. But if I am its host for too long, it will learn everything I am, discover everything I do. It will know of my connection to the Light. It would use me to destroy everything.'

'How long would it need to be in you before you lost the ability to pass it on?'

Bilis thought about this. 'I believe not more than thirty seconds. I just don't know how much longer I could fight it.'

Idris looked at Jack, then took his hand. 'Listen to me, Jack. Listen good, cos you rarely do. I'm useless to you here, I'm not part of your Torchwood gang. But let me do this. Get Bilis to use his magic whatnot to draw the Dark out of your guys and into me. They'll be free, and you'll have a better chance of defeating it. And then I'll be fine. Along with all these other people. You asked me earlier if I was "in". Yeah, yeah I am. Right in.'

Jack shook his head. 'Too risky. No.'

Bilis shrugged. 'It is a good plan. And I believe it would work.'

'The day I trust you with a friend's life is the day hell freezes over,' Jack snapped.

Gwen moved between Jack and the others, easing Idris away. 'Jack, it's a plan. It's a good plan. Stupid, too, because Idris could die, but it's his choice. You know it's the only way.'

Jack looked at Idris, then across to the painted Toshiko and Owen, standing there, utterly consumed by a power that could devastate the world.

'There's a flaw,' Ianto said. 'Idris knows our plan, too. If the Dark can read Bilis's mind, it could certainly read a weaker one like Idris's.' He glanced at Idris. 'No offense,' he said without sincerity.

Equally untruthfully, Idris replied, 'None taken.'

Jack looked at the young men. 'Boys, don't squabble over Uncle Jack, it's not very becoming.' He looked at Gwen. 'It's a risk.'

'It's all about risks. Everything we do always is.'

'He's not part of it though, is he?'

'Aren't I?' Idris asked. 'I know about you, your stupid pills don't work on me, I understand some of what's going on here. Oh, and I'm not ten years old. My choice, Jack. Ever since I met you I reckon not a lot has exactly been equal between us. So go on, give us a chance to do something. And you know what, if it goes tits up and I die, I'm not gonna complain.' He turned to Ianto. 'Mind you, it might be fun to come back and haunt you, mate.'

Before anyone could do anything, Bilis walked into the crowd. They parted slightly for him, as if recognising some great power. He took Owen and Toshiko by the hand. They started to struggle and the crowd began jostling him.

'Some help?' he cried.

Ianto, Gwen and Idris pushed people away, until Bilis and the other two were freed from the throng.

Bilis closed his eyes and squeezed Owen and Toshiko's struggling hands. The pair suddenly stopped squirming, and both staggered slightly. Bilis let go of them and opened his eyes. They were black.

Gwen moved in on Toshiko and Owen, gently steering them into 6 Coburg Street. She paused in the doorway to look back at Bilis Manger. He was motionless, Dark light playing in the sockets where his eyes should have been.

Bilis spoke. 'Idris Hopper, if you are sure…?'

Idris grabbed Bilis's hands. 'Go for it.'

The others watched in fascination as the Dark light roared out of Bilis and into Idris's violently shaking form. Idris began to scream, but the noise soon faded, leaving his mouth agape but soundless. When Bilis let go of Idris, the two men staggered away from each other.

Bilis recovered first, barking out a command. 'Get him into the house. Into my room.'

Jack reacted quickly. He scooped the prone Idris up and rushed inside the house, followed by Bilis and Ianto.

Gwen was already inside with the recovering Owen and Toshiko.

Owen lifted his head and forced open his eyes. 'Gwen?'

'Shhh,' she said. 'I'll explain everything later. First things first. We need you two to go back to the Hub. With Bilis Manger.'

Toshiko reacted now, started to ask a question, but Gwen hushed her. 'Yeah, I know, Tosh. But seriously, he's our only chance. Jack will explain it all on the way.'

She nodded over to where Jack was holding down the thrashing Idris Hopper. Idris's eyes were entirely blotted out by the Dark.

'Let's hope his head doesn't swivel and start talking about your mother,' Ianto said.

Bilis scooped up the empty prison box. 'We should leave. Now.'

'What's to stop him getting out of here after we've gone?' asked Jack uncertainly.

'His mind. Don't worry, Captain, I'll deal with it. And before you ask, no. I won't let him be hurt.'

With a last look down, Jack jumped away from Idris, who was on his feet instantly.

Ianto yanked Jack out of the room.

Bilis took one last look around him. 'Thank you,' he said, as if the room were alive. 'You kept people away successfully for so long. Goodbye.' He gave the thrashing Idris a final look, clicked his fingers and slammed the door shut. He raced out of the hall and through the front door, wrenching it shut behind him. He clicked his fingers again, and a huge metal bar, padlocked, suddenly welded itself to the front door.

'Neat,' breathed Jack.

'I swapped it for the one that's no longer at Torchwood.'

'And my private elevator? The one with the perception filter on it?'

Bilis laughed. 'My dear Jack, I'm flattered by your faith. I change perceptions, not alien realities. Your silly entrance works as it always did. You only perceived that it wasn't working, that people could see you on it. I honestly thought you'd worked that one out at least.'

Jack looked as though he wasn't sure whether to hit Bilis or not. Eventually, he just nodded to himself. 'Clever move. God, you're full of it aren't you.'

'I do hope not,' Bilis replied as they moved through the Dark-eyed crowds towards the others. 'Now, we ought to get this rigged into the Rift Manipulator. You will need to boost that aerial as soon as possible. This lot,' he pointed at the crowds, 'don't seem keen on us any more.'

Idris Hopper sat alone in the room. It was a bright room. The walls seemed to pulse with light from within, and it hurt his eyes.

All that broke up the blandness were two framed pictures, one at either end of the room. Both showed a horrible horned demon, one grey, one blue. At the foot of each beast stood an old man. The figure was neatly dressed, with a cravat, slicked-back white hair, bright eyes. The same man in each picture? A twin? A mirror image? He couldn't tell. The one with the grey demon was holding a book. The one with the blue demon had nothing.

Below the picture was a handwritten line of text:

Tretarri, Cardiff City, 1876

As he stared at the blue demon picture, the image of the man changed.

In its place, a young man, fair-haired, thin, geeky almost.

Idris suddenly realised who it was. 'No…' he muttered. Then, louder, 'No! No! No no no no no…'

Beneath it, the text of the location and date shimmered and blurred too, but he couldn't see that now, couldn't focus, because the sound of his own screams of denial filled his head, filled the room, echoing even after he'd shut up, and there was no escaping it…

TWENTY-FOUR

With a swift kick from Jack, the doorway to the top of the roof stairs gave way, flying off its hinges and skidding across the asphalt. Jack pelted through, Gwen and Ianto at his heels.

'I don't think it was locked, actually,' said Ianto.

'I wanna look cool, OK?'

Ianto made a 'whatever' with his fingers and followed the others to the dish. Jack was up and on it, already grabbing the base of the aerial.

Gwen tapped her comms. 'How're we doing, Tosh?'

Toshiko's voice echoed back to her from the Hub. 'You're doing fine, Gwen. I'm less convinced by Owen and me, frankly.'

'We've lashed the Rift Manipulator into Tosh's computer and old man Bilis there is putting the box inside,' reported Owen.

There was a beat.

'Well?' snapped Jack.

'He's not exactly one for urgency, Jack,' Owen said.

'Can he hear me?'

'Can now. I've patched the comms through to—'

'Bilis, it's Jack. I don't have time for you to mess about. Get that damn box in there and opened up.'

They heard Bilis's voice. 'It is ready.'

'So are we,' said Ianto, as he and Gwen finished connecting the cables to the aerial.

'How bloody primitive is this,' Jack muttered. 'A hundred years of alien tech, and it looks like Ianto jump-starting the SUV.'

'Oi, the SUV never needs jump-starting,' Ianto retorted.

Jack grinned. 'I just have an image in my head of you with jump leads and a pole. I was saying the SUV to save Gwen's blushes.'

'Oh don't mind me,' Gwen said. 'I gave up listening to you two hours ago. Days ago. About a year ago actually.'

'Yeah, well, some of us don't have that luxury,' Owen said in their ears. 'Thanks for the image, guys. We good to go, Tosh?' There was no verbal reply, but Owen's voice came straight back. 'Tosh gave me a thumbs up. I like to think that's Kabuki for "yes". And not "we're all gonna die in flame and devastation". But you never know, it could mean both.'

Jack sighed, pulled the box of electronic gubbins from his pocket and looked up. 'Now would be really good, guys,' he said.

Gwen was looking over the edge of the roof at the mass of black-eyed people gathered at the foot of the building, like ants. She thought for a moment of Idris Hopper, trapped in that house a few miles away, raging against all this. For all she knew, Rhys could be out there too. And all their friends, family… anyone, everyone.

Ianto joined her.

'I really, really hate heights, me,' Gwen said.

'You should go on a date with him,' Ianto said, jerking a thumb in Jack's direction. 'To him, up on a place like this, that's a great night out. But when I suggested a roller-coaster once, oh no, that was a death-trap apparently.'

Gwen laughed.

Then she stopped and looked Ianto in the eye. 'What happens now, Ianto? We saw the future.'

'We saw *a* future. A future corrupted by this Dark light stuff. In a few minutes, it'll be gone and that future won't happen.'

'How will Owen and Tosh get over this?'

'They will. Tosh will feel guilty and get introspective. Owen will never mention it again. That's their way of dealing. You?'

Gwen shrugged. 'You're right. I'll ignore it. And I'll tell Rhys that if I ever get pregnant, we'll have a home birth. Or go to Spain.'

'Guys? Please!' That was Jack.

'Jack?' And that was Tosh. 'I'm ready whenever you are.'

Jack pointed at the box of electronics at the foot of the mast and the thin wires attaching it to the aerial. 'Ready as we'll ever be.'

'Residual energy from last night's activity… connected.

It works, Jack, it works!' Toshiko coughed slightly. 'Sorry. Rift… activating… now!'

And, sure enough, above their heads, Jack, Gwen and Ianto watched the crimson ribbon of the Rift flare into existence, now bereft of extraneous light creatures.

'Hooray for us,' muttered Ianto.

Jack was at the electrics, twisting the dial Tosh had set up.

Gradually, above their heads, the Rift began to fluctuate. The ribbon of energy moved, until it was in a direct line from the top of Stadium House to the area of Tretarri.

'Now Bilis, now!' snapped Jack.

'He's gone,' Owen confirmed from the Hub.

Wharf Street, Tretarri.

A spike of Rift energy stabbed into the new concrete, and all the lights exploded. Bilis ignored the flying glass. Another ribbon of energy connected with the ground, earthing itself. The windows in every house exploded outwards, but still Bilis refused to let it affect him.

Ianto pointed west. They watched a streak of Dark light rising upwards.

'Well, that'll be Idris I guess,' Gwen said.

Jack tweaked the dials on the box. 'Let's hope we're in time,' he muttered.

And another thin black spike of raw Dark energy speared up, this one from below, shooting past them and into the Rift energy ribbon.

Ianto watched and saw the assembled citizens drop to the ground one by one, as the Dark light fled their host bodies, hungry for Rift energy.

After a minute, once the last person had dropped, the Dark light stopped pouring up.

'We're done, Tosh.'

Bilis raised the diary and began flicking through the pages faster and faster. The light creatures were escaping from the ink and being drawn into the safety of the Rift energy and back under the ground, to keep whatever existed beneath the surface caged. Their eternal task.

He noticed the face of Greg Bishop, momentarily etched amongst the lights in the Rift ribbon. It seemed... serene.

One day he might tell Jack Harkness about that.

Then again...

'Oi, Bilis,' someone shouted.

He looked up. Idris Hopper was rushing out of 6 Coburg Street, no sign of the Dark in him now. 'What's going on?'

Then Idris hit the ground. The street was shaking and, one after another, the houses of Tretarri began to crumble. The roads were splitting asunder; building after building collapsed in upon itself.

After a few moments, it was all over. The whole site was nothing more than rubble and dust.

Bilis knelt down to the ground, quite effortlessly for a man of his apparent age. He gently pushed his hand into the cracked roadway and retrieved some grey ashes.

He sniffed them, then smiled. He reached into a pocket

and pulled out a wooden box, identical to the one back at the Hub, currently filling up with the imprisoned Dark. He opened the box and deposited the grey ash inside it.

Snapping the box shut, Bilis Manger smiled and stood up again. He straightened his cravat and brushed the glass and detritus from his jacket.

'Goodbye Jack,' he said quietly. 'Until the next battle, of course.'

And he vanished into space or time or wherever it was he came from.

The diary flopped to the broken-up ground, just an old empty book.

A few flames licked up from the torn roadway, where electrical cables had been damaged. Thirty seconds later, Tretarri and the diary had combined into one massive funeral pyre to the past.

At the Hub, Toshiko was monitoring the Rift, noting the new energy racing through it, energy she'd never seen before. And hoped she never would again.

Energy that, she knew all too well, could destroy the future.

She glanced up at Bilis's wooden box in the base of the Rift Manipulator embedded in the water tower. The box seemed to be growing darker by the second.

And then the last blink of Dark energy was gone from the Rift. She closed the connection, ignoring the shower of sparks as her computer fried.

'Now!' she barked at Owen.

'Always me has to do the dangerous stuff,' he muttered as he ran across the Hub to the tower.

'We make a good team,' Toshiko murmured, more to herself than to Owen.

If he heard, he said nothing. He just slammed the lid down, turned the key and yanked the box out. 'What now?'

'Jack?'

Jack's voice came out of the ether. 'Now we get some sleep.'

'What about this box?' asked Owen, but there was no reply.

'Perhaps you should sit on it till they get back here?' laughed Toshiko.

Owen gave her a look that suggested that he didn't find the idea that funny.

Gwen knelt in front of the rubble of Tretarri and let some of it sift through her hands. She spotted a half-melted collection bucket a few paces away.

'I remember that,' she said. 'But the rest of it's fading. I can't remember the future scenario much at all now.'

Ianto opened his mouth as if to speak, but then closed it. 'No,' he said, surprised. 'Me neither.'

'Jack?'

Their leader just gave his whitest smile. 'I don't dream, remember?' he said.

'I wonder where Bilis Manger is now,' Ianto looked around.

'Who cares,' Jack said. 'We could still write what we know about him and his motives on the back of a postage stamp. Not sure I like that.'

'Well, some poor bastard at City Hall is going to have fun explaining this,' said a voice behind them.

Jack didn't turn around, just smiled. 'Idris Hopper. Saviour of the City of Cardiff.'

'And it won't be me.'

Gwen smiled at him. 'Oh go on, they might make you Mayor!'

Idris shook his head. 'Tell me, Gwen. Jack told me that his amnesia pills didn't work on you. Is it true?'

Gwen was slightly stumped at this. 'Um, well, not exactly. I mean, they would have I think, but something in my head snapped and I broke through them.'

'One in 800,000, Idris.' Jack took a bottle of pills out of his pocket. 'I just happen to be standing here with the only two I know of. Why?'

'Give me one Jack. Please. A really, *really* strong dosage. I want to wake up tomorrow not remembering any of this. Or you lot. No disrespect, Gwen, Ianto, but me and Torchwood. Don't really want to know.'

'Might not work,' Gwen said. 'No matter what strength.'

Idris shrugged. 'Another risk worth taking. Let's face it, if I'm knocking on your door in twenty-four hours, asking for a slice of pizza and a look at a Weevil, then you need to go back to your chemistry labs, Jack.'

Jack tossed him the bottle. 'Strength five is safe. For humans. Take two, Idris. And good luck.'

Idris took two pills out and threw the bottle back.

He doffed his head at Torchwood, turned and walked away, the pills still in his hand.

'Will he?' Ianto asked.

'Dunno, to be honest.' Jack smiled a little sadly. 'I hope not.'

'Because he's a useful contact?' Gwen brushed dust off her hands.

'No,' said Jack. 'I just quite enjoyed his friendship.' He sighed. 'Let's get back home. We've a box to bury in concrete.'

'You mean, *I* have a box to bury in concrete,' Ianto moaned.

'Well, I'm sure we'll help you bury it,' said Gwen.

'But *mixing* concrete?' asked Jack. 'Not these hands.'

'Nor mine,' added Gwen, linking her arm through both Jack and Ianto's as they began to walk towards Grangetown and then on to Cardiff Bay. 'And I'm sure Owen and Tosh will find better things to do…'

Three weeks later, Idris Hopper was at Bristol Airport, holdall on his shoulder. He'd checked his cases in, got his boarding pass and was about to board the 14.25 to Shoenfeld.

He looked back over his shoulder, suddenly. Didn't know why, but he felt like someone was watching him.

There was no one he knew. A couple of kids and a woman, waving goodbye to grandparents. A middle-aged lady with a briefcase passing it to a flustered businessman. A couple of other people were standing there, presumably making sure their friends or relatives got on the plane.

There was also a man, and something in Idris wondered if he'd seen him before. Dark hair, square jaw, blue eyes. Wearing a long military-style coat. Oh. He looked a bit like Tom Cruise, that must be what it was.

Idris walked onto the plane.

'Mr Hopper, *Guten Tag*. Seat 23C, window, straight down the aisle. *Danke*.'

'*Danke,*' he replied, and made his way to his seat.

Small plane, he thought. Two seats, aisle, two middle seats, other aisle, two seats, window. Nice onboard entertainment system, but it was a short flight, not much point in a movie. Might get an episode of *Frasier* or *The Simpsons* in though.

He chucked his bag in the overhead locker and settled down, watching the other passengers come aboard, hoping, as travellers always do, that no one would sit beside him.

Not that Idris minded people. But it was that natural instinct – the same on buses and trains – to hope that no one sits close by you.

Oh, bad luck.

'Ah, my seat. Good afternoon,' said his fellow traveller.

He carried nothing other than a newspaper. He sat down and smiled at Idris.

Old man, very neat and precise. Old-school English, even the cravat was there. But his eyes seemed to burn with intellect and life.

Then Idris noticed he was carrying something under the paper.

It was a small wooden box.

Second thing in fifteen minutes that had seemed somehow familiar to Idris. But a box was just a box.

The old man saw where Idris was looking.

'Sorry,' he said in a soft voice. 'I wanted to carry him with me.'

Oh. Oh, right.

'Umm, your father?'

'No,' the old man said, smiling. 'No, although in many ways, he was like one to me. No, I used to serve a very wise and wonderful master, but he died a while ago. I have only recently been trusted with my Lord's ashes and am taking them to be interred out of Britain.'

'Right. I'm sorry. Clearly he meant a great deal to you.'

'Indeed. And you, sir? Why are you travelling today?'

'Oh, me? I, well, I got a job offer. Out of the blue actually. And for some reason Cardiff felt a bit… you know, cloying after living there so many years. So I thought, hell, Idris Hopper, why not? Why not take a gamble and do something exciting with your life? So, same basic job but in a new environment.'

'You speak the language?'

'Yes. Need to in my line of work. English, German, French, Italian and a smattering of Russian. Not much Welsh, mind.'

The old man smiled at this. 'Excellent. I admire a man who can converse freely.' He shuffled in his seat. 'Well, if you will excuse me, I need to rest for a while.'

'Oh, not at all,' Idris said, secretly glad he wouldn't need to make conversation with the nice old man and his rather scary box of ashes.

The old man gave Idris one last look before turning back to his snooze.

'A pleasure to make your acquaintance, Mr Hopper. And good luck in Berlin.'

ACKNOWLEDGEMENTS

Firstly, thanks to Russell, Julie, Chris and Richard for letting me do this – and especially to Cath for being so generous about Bilis.

Thanks, too, to poor Brian, who has had to share an office with me when I've been in my darkest 'ohgodihavetowritreabookinaludicrouslyshorttime' moods; to John Roulston-Bates for his life-saving apartment and desktop in Noo Yoik; to Steve Tribe for quite amazing patience; and to Charlotte Bruton for being in my corner so readily and so often.

And, finally, to all the Torchwood TV series writers and actors who've made these characters so much fun to transfer to a different medium.

Yaaay Torchwood!

Dr Bob Strong's GP surgery has been treating a lot of coughs and colds recently, far more than is normal for the time of year. Bob thinks there's something up but he can't think what. He seems to have caught it himself, whatever it is – he's starting to cough badly and there are flecks of blood in his hanky.

Saskia Harden has been found on a number of occasions submerged in ponds or canals but alive and seemingly none the worse for wear. Saskia is not on any files, except in the medical records at Dr Strong's GP practice.

But Torchwood's priorities lie elsewhere: investigating ghostly apparitions in South Wales, they have found a dead body. It's old and in an advanced state of decay. And it is still able to talk.

And what it is saying is 'Water hag'…

Featuring Captain Jack Harkness as played by John Barrowman, with Gwen Cooper, Owen Harper, Toshiko Sato and Ianto Jones as played by Eve Myles, Burn Gorman, Naoki Mori and Gareth David-Lloyd, in the hit series created by Russell T Davies for BBC Television.

Also available from BBC Books

TORCHWOOD

TRACE MEMORY
David Llewellyn

ISBN 978 1 84607 438 7
UK £6.99 US$11.99/$14.99 CDN

Tiger Bay, Cardiff, 1953. A mysterious crate is brought into the docks on a Scandinavian cargo ship. Its destination: the Torchwood Institute. As the crate is offloaded by a group of local dockers, it explodes, killing all but one of them, a young Butetown lad called Michael Bellini.

Fifty-five years later, a radioactive source somewhere inside the Hub leads Torchwood to discover the same Michael Bellini, still young and dressed in his 1950s clothes, cowering in the vaults. They soon realise that each has encountered Michael before – as a child in Osaka, as a junior doctor, as a young police constable, as a new recruit to Torchwood One. But it's Jack who remembers him best of all.

Michael's involuntary time-travelling has something to do with a radiation-charged relic held inside the crate. And the Men in Bowler Hats are coming to get it back.

Featuring Captain Jack Harkness as played by John Barrowman, with Gwen Cooper, Owen Harper, Toshiko Sato and Ianto Jones as played by Eve Myles, Burn Gorman, Naoki Mori and Gareth David-Lloyd, in the hit series created by Russell T Davies for BBC Television.